GUARDING LEAH

BROTHERHOOD PROTECTORS WORLD

TEAM WOLF
BOOK FIVE

REGAN BLACK

Twisted Page Press LLC

*For Jen, without your brainstorming prowess and compassionate friendship I'd still be lost.
And always, with special thanks to Elle James, for inviting me into her world of Brotherhood Protectors.*

*Visit ReganBlack.com for a full list of books, excerpts, and upcoming release dates.
For free reads and much more, subscribe to Regan's monthly newsletter.*

GUARDING LEAH

TEAM WOLF BOOK 5

USA Today
Bestselling Author

REGAN BLACK

CHAPTER 1

It was murder, pure and simple. Her heart cracked, sorrow spilling through her entire body, leaving her stomach in knots and her hands balled into fists. Never easy to bear witness to a senseless death. Didn't matter that the lifeless body was four-legged rather than human. Worse yet, this was murder compounded by kidnapping.

As the hot lick of temper burned through her first layer of grief, Leah Williams silently vowed to find justice.

She'd been working undercover in and around Yellowstone National Park for months in an effort to find and break up an exotic pet ring. The secretive, criminal team had stolen young wolves, selling them to people with more money than sense as unique pets and status symbols. That was dreadful enough, considering the ongoing struggle for healthy wolf conservation, but lately, new hybrid wolf-dogs had shown up in veterinarian offices across the country.

The leads were wispy at best. As the days passed, Leah worried the case was slipping through her fingers. Most days she felt as if she were chasing ghosts and rumors that would never amount to justice for these beautiful animals.

Experience had taught her how difficult it was to overcome rumors.

Tears blurred her vision as she knelt beside the body of the dead wolf. Male, prime of his life. She swiped at her face. "I'll find them, I promise." And she would make them pay for this horrid, inexcusable destruction.

People had all sorts of opinions about gray wolf conservation. For Leah, daughter of a veterinarian and an ecology professor, the bottom line was simple: healthy predators were essential for balance within every ecosystem. Incidents like this only twisted an already delicate issue and cast more shadows over the ongoing efforts to protect the wolves.

She sniffed back another wave of tears and looked up at the hazy sky. Crying had to wait. Right now she needed clear vision to study the scene and, with luck, pick up a trail. There were prints all over, mature wolves along with the smaller tracks of younger pups. They had been ambushed as they came out of the trees.

The dead male wouldn't have led a training hunt alone, which meant it was likely other mature wolves were either wounded or had been taken along with the juveniles that fetched the highest prices for the poachers. The wolves didn't know it, but Leah was their best chance of being reunited with the pack.

It was a brazen person who shot and killed a GPS-collared wolf. The device was impossible to miss. The lure of the payout for the wolves clearly overrode all common sense. The brutality and greed of such a wasteful act scraped against everything Leah held dear.

A cold wind pushed at her as she scanned the area, trying to get a sense of how the thieves had attacked this hunting party. In addition to tracking collars, the Yellowstone Heritage Research Center used trail cameras and drone flights to locate and track the wolf packs. A drone operating a regularly scheduled sweep of the area had spotted the dead wolf. Leah had volunteered to come investigate.

She stalked back to where she'd left her ATV and pulled a camera from her supply kit. Documenting the scene took time and focus. There were tracks everywhere, including flattened areas where wolves must have sluggishly dropped from being hit with a tranquilizer. There was no sign of a dead animal laced with a sedative to lure the wolves here. For Leah that meant two shooters, minimum. One to kill, one to tranquilize. And how did they haul away the drugged wolves?

Before fury could blind her, she forced herself to find any possible silver lining. At least the wolves stolen weren't young pups. A few were surely young, but all were hearty. Every animal caught in this ambush was part of the greater pack. Each individual knew the rendezvous site and their place within the pack as a whole. And they would resume those places, those strong ties with the pack, once Leah rescued them.

Bonus, she realized, the shooters were now stuck with the difficult task of moving the heavy, unconscious grown wolves. That would slow them down, giving her a welcome advantage.

Leah cleared the emotion from her throat and chest before she radioed back to the research center. "I found the scene," she said. "One wolf dead, possibly other adults injured. Wolf tracks lead southwest. I believe several wolves are gone."

"Gone?" Bobby Tremaine was on the other end of the radio and in that one word, she heard all the sorrow she felt pressing down onto her shoulders. "You mean killed?"

"No," Leah reported. "Taken. Stolen," she clarified. "Only one wolf body is here at the scene. Very little scavenging so far."

Bobby swore. A graduate student, passionate about ecology conservation, he had joined the research team a few months before Leah. He had been operating the drone that spotted the downed wolf. "The crew was organized."

"Yes," she confirmed. "They worked quickly. At least two of them, possibly more," she added. "Though I haven't sorted out the human tracks yet." It made sense to her that the two shooters would've needed more help to move the wolves out so fast. The missing wolves probably weighed at least ninety pounds each.

"Send pictures."

The flat, no-nonsense order from him made her smile. He wasn't exactly her superior on the chain of command, but she understood the same need for justice pushed both of them. Bobby, along with pretty much everyone else in and around West Yellowstone, had been on her suspect list when she'd arrived. It hadn't taken her long to rule him out, especially with an assist from one of the research and technology specialists her actual employers kept on the payroll.

The Guardian Agency, a discreet personal protection and investigations service managed by the law firm of Gamble and Swann had reached out to her, giving her a fresh start when she'd hit rock bottom and been forced to give up her dream of becoming a veterinarian. The new career path had been an adjustment, but she liked the variety of the work and—finally—enjoyed the satisfaction of making a difference.

Since becoming a protector, most of her cases involved watching over people, but she'd leapt at the chance to intervene on behalf of the wolves.

Keeping her secrets had been easier than she'd anticipated as she adjusted and blended into the small town life of West Yellowstone. In general, the people were friendly without being too nosy and her cover story, thanks again to an agency specialist, was rock solid.

"I will. And I'll send them while I have a signal, before I move on," she promised.

"Move on? No," Bobby protested. "You need to wait for backup."

Then what had been the point of her driving out here immediately? Of course, Bobby didn't know that her interests, training, and orders went beyond her daily tasks at the center.

"Don't worry," she said. "I'm only looking for any signs of a trail. I won't go far."

"You'd better not. Weather is rolling your way," Bobby warned.

She studied the horizon, noticed the heavy gray clouds gathering. It was always a good day for snow in Yellowstone. "I'll be careful."

Weather out here could shift in a blink. Her supply kit was stocked, she had the radio, and she knew how to protect herself from human and natural threats.

The successful breeding and growth of this pack were a big win for conservation and the gray wolf population overall. She had to try and find the thieves, rescue the wolves. That was the first priority. Second was getting information. If she caught up with the thieves, caught them with the wolves, she'd have leverage that could get her to the next step of this operation. Even with the help from Guardian Agency researchers, they didn't yet have a name or likely location for the cross-breeding operation.

Rumors and ghosts. This was her best chance to change that.

"Radio is on if you need me," she told Bobby. But she was done discussing it. "Pictures on the way."

She clipped the radio back onto her belt and carefully walked another circuit of the scene. It wasn't easy. There had been more snow overnight, and a few small scavengers taking advantage of the unexpected meal. At last, Leah found a boot print near one of the subtle depressions where a wolf had been knocked out.

Oh, yeah. Taking more pictures, she spotted the bright pink tail piece of a tranquilizer dart. She photographed it carefully before she wrapped it to preserve any evidence and stowed it in her kit.

"Bastards," she grumbled. "You'll pay," she vowed to the big, wide open sky stretching overhead.

Her protection assignments had taken her to several fascinating locations. She'd enjoyed herself, but she'd simply fallen in love with this unexpectedly rugged and beautiful part of the world. When she'd taken on this assignment it had been a pure rush of wonder and joy. Working in Yellowstone was a gift in and of itself. Her parents always joked that she thrived out in the wild. A "natural-born" animal lover and perpetual champion of the underdog.

Beyond the ideal work-life balance she found in this area, she was eager to make inroads and take down the exotic pet ring. Making things right made her heart happy.

Years ago, when she'd been in a pit of despair, if anyone had told her she'd eventually be passionate about a new career with one of the best protection agencies in the business, she would have laughed hysterically.

All her life, Leah had believed she'd been destined to follow in her mother's footsteps as a veterinarian. It was a lifestyle she understood, a commitment she respected and loved. Plans changed and, though the shifting trajectory had not been her idea and had been quite painful at the time, she appreciated this new opportunity.

When she joined the Guardian Agency she never thought it would lead her to working with animals again. Protecting wolves instead of people was a unique situation, although the two went hand in hand despite the resistance to that truth. Nature conservation was vital to human survival. She was proud to have this time here alongside the people working toward a peaceful coexistence.

And she was thankful for the chance, at last, to track down the selfish killers and thieves who were attacking the wolves of Yellowstone for profit.

On her belt, her radio crackled.

"Leah? Leah, if you can hear me you need to come back to town." Bobby sounded almost panicked. "Whatever you've gathered, we'll make do."

Leah shook her head. She wasn't leaving until she had a basic direction, preferably a trail. The wolves needed her to persist. The sooner they were found, the sooner they could be reunited with the pack.

"The weather is changing, Leah," Bobby said. "You need to get back here."

"I think I've found the trail." Not a lie. She was close to figuring out where they'd gone. "I need a few minutes to confirm."

"Leah. Listen to me."

"Notify the closest airports," she said. "They'll want to get out of the area fast." The fastest way to move the animals, without keeping them sedated too long, would be by air.

"Already done," he confirmed. "Don't ignore the real issue. You need to get back here or find shelter."

She caught herself before she snapped at him. He was being responsible, trying to help. She was the one pushing the envelope. "I'll be safe, I promise."

When she was satisfied with her documentation, she uploaded the photos to the center's cloud storage and then tucked the camera into her coat. The wind had changed, kicking up with a bit of bite. Walking to the ATV, she zipped her coat against the elements. Adjusting her cap and pulling on her gloves and hood, she sat down and studied the terrain.

The thieves couldn't have moved out in just any direction. Going back to West Yellowstone would be foolish unless they had someone waiting at the airport, ready to go. The tranquilizers would keep the wolves quiet for a time, but it would be impossible to hide the transfer of several large animals from a truck to a plane. Although the gateway town didn't boast a huge population, people noticed when things were out of place. And moving wolves would stick out.

She could make Bobby happy and go back and confirm for herself that the thieves weren't at the

West Yellowstone airport. With those dark snow-filled clouds rolling closer to town, it was unlikely that a plane would escape tonight. Another drone flight wasn't going to happen until the weather passed.

Since being assigned to this particular case, she'd taken every opportunity to hike and explore the area in and around the park. Her bosses, Gamble and Swann, were aware that breaking up this particular criminal endeavor would take time. That had been another factor in sending Leah. Other than parents she visited primarily on the holidays, she didn't have deep roots or connections. After the fiasco in vet school, she didn't want to create any. These days, she trusted only a handful of people.

"A loner and happier for it" had been her motto these past few years. And this loner was ready to take down the team that had ambushed the pack.

Gray wolves were amazing creatures. Predators and opportunists? Absolutely. Also a beautiful, essential part of the food chain and the health of this corner of the planet. Intelligent animals with an admirable survival instinct.

She could relate to that focus on survival and the general plight of the wolves: being blamed for things that weren't their fault. People were set in their opinions, many of them refusing to budge or open their minds to an opposing viewpoint. Leah expected the conservationists and ranchers would be butting heads over this until the end of time, unfortunately.

The men preying on this pack were still close. Close enough to track and, hopefully, detain.

What was the fastest path away from the crime scene? She wasn't looking for the easiest route, just the option that gave the shooters room to escape.

From her perch on the ATV, she examined the surrounding area. Recalling the drone footage, matching it with the ugly scene in front of her, she searched for the best line of sight for killing this wolf. He must have tried to defend the drugged wolves somehow. Maybe a tranquilizer failed. The wolf was in his prime and would've been a good candidate for the hybrid breeders. A shooter must have been covering the approach of the thieves collecting the animals once they'd succumbed to the tranquilizer.

Starting the vehicle, she carefully advanced toward the treeline where the shooters must've been hiding, waiting for the pack to come through. The closest ridge was too far for a reliable shot with the ever-shifting winds out here.

About one hundred yards east of the deadly ambush, she noticed something more than the boot prints closer to the scene. The flat slide resembled a toboggan track and had been cleverly used to hide most of the evidence of the shooters. Only a rare boot print remained uncovered, but now that she knew what she was looking for, she had an easy time trailing after them.

She inched along following the path that became more evident as she reached the treeline. Two people, men based on the size of the boots, had worked hard maneuvering the heavy sleds through the trees.

Stopping the ATV once more, she radioed back to update Bobby. "I've picked up the trail. They retreated east into the trees. Sedated wolves on sleds covered the tracks."

"So not headed to the airfield here in town," Bobby said.

"Not directly." She wasn't ready to rule out anything just yet. Two people couldn't keep the sedated wolves indefinitely. There was a handoff point somewhere. A place they could load the wolves into some kind of vehicle to haul them out of the park. "I'm going to follow a bit more."

"Leah. The weather."

"It's not here yet." She didn't want Bobby's worry weighing her down. All her energy and focus had to be on the task ahead. "I've got this." Leah couldn't give up, not when she was this close to finally getting a photo or a name to connect with this dangerous crew.

Her gaze returned to the evidence of the trail. Shoving her anger down deep, she headed into the trees after the thieves. Though it slowed her down, she paused frequently to take pictures and scan the area, listening for any threat. She couldn't rule out the possibility that they'd left someone to guard the trail. She pressed forward, taking the calculated risk that the thieves would be more intent on getting away than protecting their exit.

The little intel they'd gathered on the operation pointed to a small, discreet group. Maybe three or four people, probably men, working sporadically when called upon. They had one grainy photo of a man—white, mid-twenties, lanky, in a truck with stolen Montana plates—delivering a hybrid puppy to a family at a rest stop north of Des Moines, Iowa.

Leah had been sure she'd seen a man bearing a striking resemblance to the grainy photo in West Yellowstone last week. So, no, she wasn't giving up this chase. There was no telling when she'd be this close to such a valuable lead again.

When her path was blocked by fallen trees, Leah parked the ATV. Taking the radio and a small pack that included her personal handgun, she followed on foot rather than move too far off the trail and lose it.

Over the logs, moving slowly, the sound of her footsteps were swallowed by the soft, snow-covered ground. She peered up at the frosted white tree limbs tangled overhead. The drone wouldn't have found a small ambush team in here unless they'd known exactly where to look.

A loud crack shattered the eerie quiet. Leah jumped back, pressing close to a tree trunk as an icy limb crashed to the ground, kicking up a spray of stinging snow and debris.

Dusting herself off, she took a breath and resumed her search.

The next sound was the burst of gunfire. Leah dropped to the forest floor, scrambling to find cover as her heart pounded.

"Make sure she's dead!" a voice shouted.

A moment later an engine rumbled to life in the distance. Leah held her breath, listening for any clue to the shooter's position. Hearing him grumbling about the weather, she waited for an opening, no matter how slim.

Then she ran.

WADE FIELDING SCALDED his tongue on his piping hot coffee as he leaned against the porch railing of the Grand Yellowstone Lodge in West Yellowstone. The morning air had a crisp bite, reminding him of winters back home in Lake Placid. As a kid, a day like this one would've found him heading to Whiteface for a day on the ski slopes with his best friend Justice Kane.

He and Justice had grown up together. More than friends, they'd become brothers forged through hardships and high points. Justice had been determined to get out of town and Wade wouldn't let him go alone, so they'd joined the Army together right out of high school. For years, they'd served side by side, adding yet another layer to their history as brothers from different mothers. When it was time, they'd left the Army and their last assignment with the 10th Mountain in Fort Drum. Now they found themselves in West Yellowstone along with Gabe, Nate, and Alex, the other three members of their team.

Hank Patterson, founder of the Brotherhood Protectors and Stone Jacobs, leader of the newly formed Yellowstone division, had made the five of them an intriguing offer packed with challenges that fit their passion for search and rescue to a tee. Hesitant at first, it hadn't taken long for all of them to feel all-in and part of the new community as a whole.

Wade didn't have any complaints. He loved the area, the work, and the people he'd come to call his friends. Still, it was strange to be the last man from 10th Mountain still calling the lodge home after the other guys had moved on. One by one, Gabe, Nate, Alex, and Justice had fallen in love with amazing, talented, and brave women. Somehow, each one of them had known they'd met the right woman and leapt into that happy ever after commitment.

Wade sipped his coffee, imagining Justice striking a similar pose out at Payton's house this morning. Well, it wasn't just her place anymore. She and Justice were a team, start to finish, and as happy as Wade was for his brother, it all felt a bit surreal.

He hadn't even been sure his brother believed in romantic love. Although Wade's parents had been a positive example of love at work and the Fielding family remained strong even after his dad's death, Justice's childhood home had been one nightmare after another. There had been relationships, but Justice had always skirted along the edge, avoiding anything resembling a serious commitment.

Wade studied the horizon. Sipped his coffee. They'd had snow overnight and everything looked pristine and fresh. He found the view full of promise and possibilities, even if the sun was obscured by thick cloud cover. Any day that began with a quiet, deep breath outside was off to a good start.

Behind him, he heard the front door swing open and smiled to himself.

"You should come on in and grab some breakfast before it's gone," John Jacobs said.

As the father of Stone Jacobs and owner of the Grand Yellowstone Lodge, John supported his son's division of the Brotherhood Protectors by offering rooms to team members coming to the area. Although he'd refurbished the lodge to serve guests from all over the country, most of the action around the place lately revolved around the new venture.

"Won't be surprised if we have some trouble today," Wade said, his words creating small vapor clouds between them.

"No argument from me." John shook his head. "People always underestimate the weather. it can change on a dime out here."

Not just here. Wade's thoughts sifted through some of the more memorable of his search and rescue efforts in the Army and as a civilian. If there was one constant in Wade's experience, it was that Mother Nature was fickle on the best of days.

Last night Wade had gone out to the airport for a standby shift and listened in on a couple of emergency calls.

The storm had rolled in, dropping snow from heavy clouds with a vengeance and gone on its merry way almost as quickly. Made for a pretty landscape and caused misery for campers who had been caught in the elements without the right cold weather gear or equipment.

Following John inside, Wade helped himself to the hearty breakfast Cookie had whipped up for the lodge's guests. A former chef on the USS Carl

Vinson aircraft carrier, the man seemed to work culinary magic no matter the meal, the menu, or the number of people who needed to be fed.

Working his way through a plate filled with bacon, scrambled eggs, and fluffy biscuits, Wade watched Stone walk in. The hair on the back of his neck lifted the way it always did when trouble found him. Taking one last bite of eggs and polishing off a slice of bacon, he quickly finished his coffee.

His new boss wore a grave expression that matched the somber mood of the people behind him. Ben Yates, one of Stone's teammates who helped establish the Brotherhood Protectors here, held hands with his lady. Chelsea Youngblood, Wade recalled. She studied the local wolves at the Yellowstone Heritage Research Center.

"How are you feeling this morning?" Stone asked.

Wade stood and started to clear his plate. "Always ready."

"Take it easy," Stone said. "I know you were on standby at the airfield overnight. I can call in someone else."

"No need." Wade glanced at Ben. "If I wasn't ready, I'd say so. Where am I headed?"

Chelsea swallowed and she leaned closer to Ben.

Wade got a bad feeling in the pit of his stomach. He suddenly wished he'd skipped the bacon.

"A member of our research team didn't come back yesterday." She paused, took a breath. "She went out to investigate an anomaly we spotted during a regular drone flight. We have a GPS location on the ATV she was using, but we haven't been able to get eyes on it." Chelsea lifted her chin. "Radio contact ended just before the storm hit. Bottom line, I'm sure she's in trouble and I need someone to go find her."

"They sent a drone up at first light over her last known location," Ben added. "ATV is deep into the trees. Impossible to get a read on the situation."

"I'll find her," Wade assured them. What qualified as a wolf anomaly? "Can I see that footage? Get a look at any information you have?"

"Absolutely," Stone said. "We've got it all queued up for you in the barn."

Since leaving military service, Wade and his team had assisted with many civilian search and rescue efforts close to home in and around the Adirondacks. They'd trained others and consulted with various park services and first responders. In Yellowstone, Wade discovered they did all of that and more.

"Let's go." He didn't want to waste any time.

If the researcher had been out all night in the storm, this might quickly shift from rescue to recovery. He followed Stone, Ben, and Chelsea out the back door to the barn that had been modified for Brotherhood Protector purposes.

He sat down in front of a monitor, and watched footage they had ready for him.

After reviewing it a few times, Wade asked Stone, "Can Justice take me up in the helo? I'd like an overhead view."

With a nod, Stone reached for his phone. "On it."

"What's her name and what was she doing out there?" Wade asked Chelsea.

"Her name is Leah Williams," Chelsea replied. "She went out to check on the wolf pack after a drone flight spotted what appeared to be a dead wolf on one of the usual hunting paths."

"You're serious." Shock settled over him. He set the drone footage to play once more, but there wasn't much evidence of trouble. Other than the stationary wolf. Healthy wolves didn't drop dead all by themselves in this area. "Could there have been some sort of fight within the pack?"

"Not that the drone operator witnessed. He told me Leah was certain the pack had come under attack." Chelsea swallowed. "Seems she was right."

"Damn poachers." The criminals taking advantage of animosity toward the wolves seemed to be a persistent threat. One Wade had grossly underestimated. Wolves were protected, but in the months since he'd arrived in Yellowstone, it seemed those protections were fragile and frequently ignored. It annoyed his overall sense of fairplay and justice. Not to mention it was outright offensive to upset the ecosystem and balance of wildlife.

"Not poachers, exotic pet traders." Chelsea's fingers curled around the back of the chair next to Wade, hard enough to turn her knuckles white. "I'm afraid of what happened to her overnight. We couldn't send the drone to cover her, due to the incoming weather."

Stone returned, turning his phone around in his hands. "Justice is inbound. He'll be waiting at the airport."

"Great. I'll be ready." Wade had confidence in his tracking skills. In his opinion, only Nate's dog, Pierce, was better. "Where are the radio transcripts?"

"Here." Ben handed him a few loose pages.

Wade read through the all-too-brief exchanges. "This is it?" He scowled, reading them slower the second time through.

"Unfortunately, yes. We didn't hear from her again," Chelsea said. "All attempts to reach her have failed."

Wade turned to Chelsea. "Sum it up for me, please. What do you think happened?" If Leah had been out in the storm overnight without any protection her life was hanging in the balance by now.

Chelsea dipped her chin to the transcript. "I think she went after the men who stole those wolves. To save them from the pet traders."

"You don't think she's cooperating with the thieves?" Wade drummed his fingers on the desktop. "That would be a logical explanation for her radio silence after moving away from the scene."

"No." Stone shook his head. "I received a call from another security agency this morning. Apparently, Leah has been in West Yellowstone working undercover for the Guardian Agency. Her assignment is to find and identify the crew supplying a black market exotic pet dealer. They reached out to me when she didn't check in on schedule."

"Is she the type to try and take them down on her own?" Wade wondered. At Chelsea's nod, his respect for a woman he'd never met increased significantly. "Well, A for dedication, but is she capable?"

"Guardian Agency doesn't employ slouches," Stone said.

"Undercover or not, she's been an asset at the research center," Chelsea said, her voice cracking. "We have to find her before she gets hurt."

Ben slipped his arm around her shoulders. Wade tried not to freak out over the tenderness between them. Not his problem and definitely not his place to judge what worked for other people. His track record with romance was rocky at best.

His dad and mom had often told the story about how they'd met and fallen hard, practically at first sight. The engagement had been short, but the marriage long and happy, up until his dad died way too early. Grief had altered his opinions on love. While his mom said she wouldn't change a thing about her life, that she'd treasured every minute, Wade couldn't imagine being the source of that much heartache for anyone.

He had Justice and that was enough of a deep relationship for Wade. They were best friends, closer than brothers, and, according to their Army pals, "work-wives". He hadn't met a woman who flattened him like a steamroller, to use his dad's phrase.

Justice had. Wade loved Payton like a sister, especially the way she brought out the best in his brother. One of these days, they'd have to get his mom out here to meet her in person.

Chelsea reached around him and pointed at the screen with a map of Yellowstone and a few markers. "That pin is the location of her ATV." She moved her finger slightly. "This is the location of the last radio call."

Inside the trees. She must've been following something. "How many hours ago?" he asked.

Chelsea's hopeful expression faded. "About a half hour before the storm hit hard."

"What's her wilderness training?" Wade was still concerned this would become a recovery mission rather than a rescue.

"Leah was new to this area, but a quick learner. Excellent with directions. She had an obvious affinity for animals and a passion for the outdoors tempered by a healthy respect for the risks and dangers. I got the impression there is some vet school in her background, but she doesn't talk much about what happened before she came here."

Was that reticence due to being undercover or was Leah hiding something more? Wade hoped her healthy respect for the environment wasn't smothered by her determination to close the case.

"Do you need help gearing up?" Stone offered, cutting into his thoughts.

Wade requested an ATV, selected a rifle and two handguns from the armory, then added ammunition and cold weather gear to a short list. "If you can drop all of this at her last known location, I can pick up her trail when I finish the flyover with Justice."

"Consider it done," Stone assured him.

"Chelsea can go with you in the helo," Ben suggested. "She's an excellent spotter."

Wade shook his head. "No, thanks." He couldn't speak freely with Chelsea listening. And if they ran into trouble, he didn't want to worry about keeping Chelsea safe too. "I need to make an objective survey. Then Justice can leave me at the ATV and I can track her down."

"Just bring her back, please," Chelsea pleaded.

Wade nodded and headed out, refusing to make a promise he couldn't keep. His rescue record was impeccable. He was confident he could bring Leah back. Time would tell if that was dead or alive.

CHAPTER 2

Leah was shivering from head to toe. She rubbed her hands together and stamped her feet. Adrenaline had kept her going through the night, but she was closing in on absolute exhaustion. A headache and sore muscles only made her angry. With herself, mainly. She'd been cocky, so focused on the chase that she'd let the shooter get the drop on her.

More annoying, she'd lost her radio in the mad scramble to escape. In the darkness, with heavy wet snow coming down, she hadn't dared doubling back to look for it. Finding shelter had been her immediate concern. Hard to do her job if she died. The only upside was the fresh snow hiding her tracks from the shooter.

Without tools, she'd had to get creative. Survival out here without the proper gear was down to luck, especially in a snowstorm. She'd improvised an igloo, burrowing into the cavity left by a fallen tree, her back pressed to the root ball that extended over her head. This morning, she was all but invisible, if bitterly cold. Still no signal for her cell phone and the battery was nearly dead.

Her best hope was that the storm had deterred the shooter and sent him back to his crew, regardless of his orders to kill her. There might be some vague honor among thieves, but the weather couldn't be ignored. No one wanted to linger outside in a nasty storm. That gave her a slim advantage. If she didn't turn into a popsicle first.

"Think positive," she murmured to herself.

She'd made it through the night. Survival was in itself the spark to get her fired up and energized for the chase ahead. She had to rescue those wolves and get some actionable intel on the crew. Though she was desperate to bolt out of her hiding place and make a run for it, she waited.

Creeping forward to the edge of her makeshift shelter, she held her breath, listening. On a snow-covered morning, every sound was bright and sharp in the brittle air, held close by the thick cloud cover. Birds were stirring, morning chirps and songs getting underway with no apparent distress over a threat or something out of place.

Her narrow view of her surroundings revealed a muted, white washed landscape. It would've been beautiful, if she'd been out here for anything other than an outright hunt.

In the distance, she heard the steady low beat of a helicopter rotor. Way too early for one of the flight-seeing tours. Her heart jolted. That sound would've been a beacon of hope for a timely rescue under different circumstances. Today it felt more like a magnet for danger. If the crew was still close, they might attack whoever was up there. She held her position, hidden by the snow.

She resisted the urge to reveal herself as the helicopter cruised by overhead. None of her intel indicated the crew had this kind of asset. Then again, to the best of her knowledge no one had been so close on their heels before. As the sound faded, she prayed the pilot would keep going, away from her and on to a completely unrelated destination.

No luck. The helicopter returned and soon it was evident the pilot was working a deliberate search pattern. Right over her position.

Friend or foe? She had no way to be certain. The ATV had a GPS tag and her co-workers at the research center would be concerned that she didn't return last night. With Chelsea Youngblood's connections, it was possible they had a search underway already.

Still, she couldn't shake off the trepidation, not after being shot at last night. If she rushed out into the nearest clearing and tried to get the pilot's attention she could very well draw fire again.

As the helicopter executed another pass, she crept out of her hiding place for a better look, determined to take action if she recognized a search and rescue emblem. Even if the helo turned out to be linked to the thieves, information like the tail number would be helpful to the overall investigation.

Responsibility to her assignment and the conservationists who were so passionate about the wolves drove her to her feet. Her knees protested after being crouched for so long in the cold, but she pressed forward. As quickly and quietly as possible, Leah moved from one tree trunk to another, craning her neck for a glimpse of the helicopter.

The aircraft swept right overhead, the rotorwash stirring the branches of the tall trees. She caught the first part of the tail number before the helicopter swung out and away.

She started for the clearing, hoping to get lucky on the next passover. Another gunshot cracked through the air, sending birds into a tizzy and destroying what had been a peaceful start to the morning.

Leah swore under her breath as she dove for cover. She didn't know if the shot had been aimed at her or the helicopter. Either way, she could be confident the helicopter was on her side. And that the shooter chasing her was impatient.

Taking aim at an aircraft would definitely bring down some kind of official response to the area. Too bad she couldn't hunker down until the authorities arrived. She needed to find another hiding place. Fast.

WADE SCOURED THE GROUND BELOW, with and without binoculars, while Justice handled the helicopter. The flight was quick to the location that had drawn Leah's attention yesterday. Once they reached the ATV signal, Justice began a standard search grid.

Everything was blanketed by fresh snow and despite his expertise and vigilance he wasn't seeing an obvious trail to search. "ATV is inside the tree line," he said through the headset.

"Might've had an accident," Justice said.

"True. But why not radio for help?"

Justice snorted. "We both know terrain messes with communications. And a cell signal can go from great to non-existent in a blink out here."

Also true. Last night's snow would have been a tough survival challenge for Leah. In his opinion, the ATV inside the trees increased the odds of her finding some sort of shelter from both the weather and the wildlife.

As Justice turned back toward the ATV position, Wade hoped for some sign of Leah. There was no trace of movement, no sign of a campfire, no movement along the edge of the trees.

"Feels like a hard ask sending someone out here alone and undercover," Wade said. "Have you ever met her?"

"No." Justice scanned the horizon and his instruments. "Plenty of people jump on the tough assignments. Present company included."

"Stone and Chelsea are sure she's on the right side of this. What if they're wrong?"

"Then I suspect you'll figure that out soon enough."

"Think about it," Wade pressed. "This is the perfect cover. Feed the crew the best intel, come out right behind them and waltz right out of the park with a few blackmarket wolves."

"Possible, but unlikely," Justice replied, unruffled.

"People sell out all the time for any number of reasons." Granted, Wade didn't know Leah, but greed and desperation were ugly motivators.

"So call headquarters and ask someone to dig into her finances," Justice suggested. "Why is this getting to you?"

Without a ready answer, Wade ignored the

question, putting the binoculars to his eyes and leaning as far as he could for a clear view.

If she'd actually spent the night out here, there should be evidence of a fire. Would've been about the only way to avoid hypothermia during a snowstorm. There was nothing. The ATV was equipped with flares and an emergency kit. If she was down there, in need of a rescue, she should've fired a flare by now.

"Go ahead and set me down where they left my gear," Wade said. "She's either too injured to signal or long gone."

"You got it." Justice circled around, heading west once more.

Wade radioed headquarters with the update, knowing they'd be disappointed that he hadn't found any sign of Leah. "I'll be landing in a few minutes and then heading out on the ATV for a ground search."

"Copy," Stone replied. "Your gear is in place."

Wade started to reply when gunfire interrupted. Justice took evasive action, climbing up and away from the danger. Wade leaned into the movement, letting his brother manage the immediate crisis.

Justice swore. "You see anything?"

"No," Wade grumbled. "Small arms. Three shots, maybe four. From the trees." Questions raced through his mind, wondering what that surprising attack meant for Leah. Was she in danger or worse?

"Call it in," Justice ordered.

Wade reported the situation. "Probably an aggravated birdwatcher," he said, hoping to draw a laugh from Justice. "You're too far from the ridge and there's no other movement."

"Let's hope." His brother remained grim, his mouth set in a hard line.

"Take the long way home once you drop me off," Wade said. "I don't want to worry about you while I'm searching for Leah."

"I can take care of myself," Justice said, relaxing by small degrees. "Call me if you get in over your head."

Wade snorted a short laugh. "If that ever happens, it'll be a first."

THE HELICOPTER WAS GONE, wisely retreating from the gunfire. The earlier quiet returned, sifting between the trees to settle as thick and cold as the fresh snow. With it came a stark loneliness. The helicopter's appearance had been a big question. She hadn't known if she had a possible ally until the shots were fired. A flash of hope, quickly doused. It was up to her now. To survive and to rescue those wolves.

She had to focus. Find a way to gain an advantage. Starting with the shooter lurking out here somewhere. He was clearly determined to fulfill the order to kill her, but surely she knew the area better than an occasional wildlife thief.

The lack of sleep and the continued exposure to the cold would catch up with her quickly. Though instinct pushed her to try and recover her ATV, it was likely the shooter would expect that. Logically, a run back to West Yellowstone was her best chance of survival. However, the crew was heading east with their stolen wolves. Her temper over the audacity of the crew gave her a much-needed energy boost to keep moving despite the steep odds of the moment. Going against her basic survival instincts, Leah forced herself toward the east. Her boots crunched loudly on the snow and a glance over her shoulder showed a clear trail in her wake. She might as well be waving a flag and inviting the shooter over for hot cocoa and murder.

Her stomach growled as she picked her way along, doing her best to move quietly, placing her feet where she might leave less of a trail. A hard task right now. She paused frequently to listen for any sound of pursuit, but it was nearly impossible due to her pulse pounding in her ears. The only silver lining was knowing if the shooter had also been out here all night, he couldn't be feeling much better than her.

Could she make him give up? Lure him into a trap? At this point any offense was better than none. If she could get the upper hand with the shooter, subdue him somehow, she'd have more options. He had to have a radio, some way to stay in contact with the other members of his crew. Energized, she stopped worrying about the trail she left behind, stopped worrying about being quiet, and hurried through the trees, looking for the right spot to stage an ambush.

WADE'S TEMPER nearly boiled over as he studied the scene around Leah's ATV. It was the third strike of sorts, after being shot at and then examining the site where the wolves had been attacked.

What on earth had possessed her to chase after danger all by herself? He'd heard Chelsea sing Leah's praises and Stone's reassurance that she was one of the good guys, but her decisions made no sense. No person in their right mind would give chase armed with only a cell phone and radio as a storm rolled in. The undercover story had to be a ruse. She must be cooperating with the wolf-stealing crew on some level.

Looking around her abandoned ATV, his theory seemed even more likely. Despite the cover of snow, he recognized how she'd gotten caught on a tangle of fallen branches and debris. She'd tried to maneuver and only jammed up the front wheels, tipping over the vehicle. The emergency kit had been left behind, though he didn't see any sign of the radio. He unhooked his own device from his belt and made a couple of calls on the channel used by the research center, hoping to use his signal to find her radio.

He found her radio within minutes. Disgusted with how she'd fooled so many people, he stalked back to the overturned ATV to share the current update and his opinion on why she hadn't returned to the research center. His gaze caught the bright slash of bark stripped from a tree and Wade stopped short. Reconsidered.

The damage to the tree was fresh. Nothing natural about it. He searched until he found the bullet lodged in another tree a few yards away. He used his cell phone to take several pictures, then he dug out the bullet, slipping it into an inner pocket of his coat. Hopefully, the authorities in West Yellowstone would find some useful evidence.

He checked his cell phone signal and called Stone rather than radio in. He didn't want anyone else listening in just yet. "Found the ATV," he said when Stone picked up.

"Any sign of her?"

Not good signs. "Someone shot at her. Looks to me like she overturned the ATV in an effort to escape. Haven't found where she spent the night."

"And someone fired on you and Justice a few hours ago."

"I remember," Wade muttered.

"You want back up?" Stone asked. "We can have more boots on the ground within an hour."

Wade rarely turned down help, especially with lives on the line. This time he figured he could move faster on his own. "Let me find her first," Wade replied. He didn't want to bring out the whole team and expose them to a gunman if Leah had died.

Stone seemed to understand what Wade refused to say. "All right. She's tough, Wade."

He hoped so. Anything less than tough wouldn't have survived the night. "I collected and documented the one bullet I found. Do what you can to keep this quiet for now."

"Tell me why I'd do that."

Wade bristled. After working with only his team as private consultants, he was still adjusting to the new chain of command in the Yellowstone Brotherhood Protectors. He took a breath. Stone's request wasn't a challenge based on ego or a power play. That's not how the man worked. Wade took a breath. "Think of it as preserving the scene," he said. "I'd rather not have anyone else in here until we know the area is safe and secure." Justice evading gunfire had been enough of a stress test today.

"Your case, your call," Stone confirmed. "Good luck."

"Thanks," Wade ended the call and zipped his cell phone back into his coat.

Wade cautiously searched the area, thinking of the timing of her last radio exchange with the research center, estimating how far she might have traveled. On the ATV and on foot. Under fire, she must've been in a panic about finding cover. It wasn't easy to see a trail after the snowfall, but that's why he was here. To find a woman he didn't know, dead or alive.

When he came across evidence of a fresh campfire, his initial thought was that Leah had been here. But these boot prints were bigger. Definitely a man's shoe. He took pictures using his own foot for reference and continued on, picking up his pace.

He battled down a wave of futility as he searched. It all felt too much like guesswork as he wove his way through the trees, looking for a spot that would've sheltered a woman running scared in a snowstorm. Instinct or blind luck, he found a hollow created by a fallen tree. The snow had been compressed, pine boughs had been gathered close. She must've spent the night here.

"Definitely tough," Wade said to himself. And smart. This small pocket of safety would've put her out of sight of the gunman tracking her once the storm started and darkness fell.

Why though? If they had the wolves and had isolated the woman pursuing them, why come back for her?

He wasn't a psychologist, but greed, pride, or arrogance topped Wade's list of reasons. Maybe Leah, working undercover, had come closer than she'd known to the heart of the criminal operation. He inched along on the ATV, moving east. Eventually, he found the trail again. Leah, based on the smaller stride and size of the prints left in the snow. Still eastbound and alone as far as he could tell.

Frustrated with his slow search and mounting questions, he took a break and tried to put himself in her shoes.

He radioed back to Stone. "I believe Leah survived the night," he reported.

"Say again." Stone's voice was flat, as if he couldn't believe it.

"I believe she's still ali—"

A wild scream cut off his report. He slammed the radio down and put the ATV into gear picking his way as quickly as possible toward the source of that bone-chilling sound.

The engine drowned out the noise so that the first thing he saw was the fight.

Two people just inside the trees were facing off.

He recognized the research center logo emblem on the back of Leah's coat and assumed she was fighting the gunman who'd shot her ATV last night. Likely the same gunman who'd taken shots at the helo this morning.

But where was the gun?

Answers had to wait as her opponent kicked up snow and then lunged, tackling Leah and pinning her to the ground. With a shout, Wade cut the engine and ran to help her. Neither Leah nor her opponent seemed to hear him. She knocked the man back with a two-handed blow to his jaw and scrambled out of reach. When she popped up to her feet, she brandished a thick limb like a weapon.

"On your knees," she shouted at her attacker.

"You first," the man shot back, a sneer in his voice. He circled her, looking for an opening.

Wade pulled his gun. "Do as she says," he ordered.

Leah and her attacker both gawked at him. "Who the hell are you?" she demanded.

"A friend," he replied. "Put down the branch."

"Not a chance," she vowed. "Lower your gun."

"Is he armed?" Wade asked.

"Not at the moment," she confirmed.

Wade slowly lowered his handgun toward the holster. The other man rushed Leah, hands high, reaching for her throat. She swung the limb like a bat, catching him hard in the midsection. When he dropped she hit him again, toppling him to his side. Wade wasn't sure if the crack he heard was wood or bone.

Bone, definitely bone. He smothered a cringe when she brought the limb down forcefully once more. The man cried out, cursing and promising revenge and worse against Leah.

"Oh, poor baby. You won't be able to shoot anyone or anything for a long time."

"So I'm guessing he's not your partner," Wade observed.

"God no. What gave you that idea?"

"Had to be asked," he said.

"Did it?"

He found the absolute offense on her face almost amusing. "Nevermind." Wade inched closer, worried about spooking her. "Take it easy. Take a breath."

She aimed her full attention on him, her brown eyes glittering with a dangerous combination of adrenaline and fury. "Who are you?"

"Friend," he repeated, reluctant to reveal too much information in front of her attacker. "Stone Jacobs sent me to find you." He'd purposely used his new boss's name, primarily to reassure Leah. A dark satisfaction shot through him to see shock and fear on the injured man's face.

Wade knelt, deceptively relaxed. "Must be from

West Yellowstone if you know that name. What are you doing out here?"

"He stole wolves and has orders to kill me." Leah set the limb aside long enough to take the man's radio and search his pockets. "No ID."

"Not surprising." Wade cocked his head. "Let me see the arm."

The man curled up, trying to scoot out of reach. "She broke it."

"Closest help is West Yellowstone," Wade said. "What's your name?"

"She tried to kill me," the man snapped. "I don't know anything about any wolves. I'm just hunting."

"Big game? Helicopters maybe?"

The man swore.

Wade was running out of patience. "Who hired you? Give me a name."

"I-I can't. They'll kill me for not, um, killing her."

Maybe it was the pain or the growing fear, but the man didn't strike Wade as a cold-blooded killer. Shooting a woman was a big leap from taking out a wolf.

"Who is 'they'?" Leah grabbed the man's coat and gave him a shake that had his eyes rolling back in his head. "Answer me."

Wade nudged her aside and eased the man down to the frozen ground. "He's passed out. Probably for the best, considering that arm."

She stood, moving back to lean against a tree trunk, taking deep breaths. "You work for Stone Jacobs?"

"That's right. Wade Fielding, part of the new search and rescue group."

Her chin jerked in a nod. "You worked in the Adirondacks and the Army before that. 10th Mountain. Your team has an excellent success record."

"I'd be flattered if I wasn't a little creeped out. How do you know all that? I didn't know your name until this morning."

She lifted one hand, gave a weary wave. "Leah Williams, woman of many talents."

Research was clearly one of those talents. But why?

"His gun fell into the trap," she said.

The woman kept knocking him off balance. "What trap?"

She pointed. "Over there. Not far."

"Why don't you take a seat," he suggested. She looked as if she might fall over any second. He didn't need two unconscious people out here. "I'm going to call this in."

"Okay." She sat down, her eyes closed as she rested against the tree. "Fine."

He hurried back to the ATV and pulled a roll of duct tape and an emergency blanket from the pack. He bound the shooter's ankles and then secured his good arm to his body so he couldn't escape.

The blanket he tucked around Leah, patting her shoulder. Her eyelids fluttered open. "Relax. Just for a minute."

"Need to keep moving," she protested. "Find the wolves."

She was exhausted and dehydrated. "In a minute." He returned to the ATV for water before searching for the trap and gun. "Sip slowly," he instructed, pressing the bottle into her hands.

He found the trap easily enough, following the evidence of their fight. The tracks in the snow and the multitude of bent and broken branches led him to a spot where she'd managed to trip up the man. A rifle and a small all-weather pack were left behind. He brought the items with him as he rejoined Leah.

She was holding the man's radio in both hands. "They want an update."

"Give it to me." Wade held out a hand. "Drink some more water." He watched her eyes as she debated her options. "Telling them you're alive isn't the right play."

"Why not? I need to find those wolves."

Apparently, Chelsea had been right on target about Leah's commitment. Wade found her dedication appealing. "Only brings more heat down on you."

"Heat would be nice," she muttered.

Wade smothered a chuckle. "I bet." He wiggled his fingers. "Trust me with his radio."

She handed over the device. "If Stone trusts you, I guess I can too."

Her obvious skepticism bothered him. Most of the time, when he rescued a stranger, they were distinctly happy to see him. People usually found his presence and confidence reassuring. Leah clearly was not most people.

His frustration with that had to wait as someone on the other end of the radio call sounded angry. "Ronnie, check in damn it."

Wade paused, then clicked the mic. "I got her," he improvised a pained voice. "Broke my arm, but she's down for good."

Leah was glaring daggers at him. He held up a palm, hoping she'd stay quiet.

"Can you wait for me? This arm is—"

"No." Wade gave a start at the new voice, male and hard as granite. "We aren't waiting. You messed up, you handle it."

"Not an affectionate bunch," he said. "But we have a name." He turned to study Ronnie. The man really should've come around by now. "How are you feeling?"

"Better." Leah held out a hand and he pulled her to her feet. "Got anything to eat?"

He had rations on the ATV, but he was curious

about Ronnie's pack. Unzipping the smaller compartment, he found a couple of granola bars, a package of toaster pastry, and a flask. Wade opened it, sniffed. "Whisky."

She rolled her eyes, but held out her hand. After wiping the lip she took a long swig, then screwed the top on once more.

"Have a chaser," he suggested, handing her the pastry.

"Breakfast of champions," she said, ripping open the foil.

He appreciated her survival instinct. Food was fuel right now. Leaving the gun, pack and both radios with Leah, he walked over to Ronnie. "Ronnie." He carefully roused him. "Your pals called. Said you're on your own."

The man didn't seem surprised, refusing to make eye contact.

"Answer my questions and we'll get you some professional help."

"Right. You're just gonna leave me here."

"Not how we roll," Wade said.

"Even if it is what you deserve," Leah called out. "His pals are long gone," she added. "I haven't heard an engine nearby all day."

"Tell me how this works, man," Wade urged. "You come in, scoop up a few wolves and then what? Help me help you."

Ronnie snorted. "Not a chance."

Wade looked over his shoulder at Leah. She was rooting through Ronnie's pack. "Find anything interesting?"

"A GPS device for hikers." Her lips curled into a fierce smile as she held it up. "He has two locations marked as favorites."

The man groaned. Wade squeezed his good shoulder. "You've been very helpful, Ronnie." He stood up and walked back to Leah.

"Fitting as it might be, you can't leave him out here in the elements," she said, her voice low enough that she wouldn't be overheard.

Wade shook his head. "No, but I'm not in the mood to give him any further comfort." He plucked his radio from his belt and called in an update. Stone promised to have someone out there to pick up Ronnie as soon as possible. Wade figured with clear weather it would be within an hour. Checking the GPS device, he gave the precise coordinates.

"Leah?" Stone asked. "Is there anyone I can call for you?"

Her eyebrows shot up and her gaze darted away from Wade. "No, thanks. I'll take care of that myself."

Wade managed not to react.

"We'll look forward to seeing you," Stone said. "Chelsea will be relieved to hear you're okay."

With the radio call finished, Wade said, "Ready to go?"

Leah's lips parted and her dark eyebrows flexed into a frown, but Ronnie's voice cut her off. "You can't leave me here," he shouted. "I have rights."

"You won't be waiting long," Wade promised. "Someone else can go over your rights. I'm not arresting you, I'm neutralizing a predator."

"You're making a mistake," Ronnie said. "I can make you rich. Name your price. Let me go and you can name your price."

"As if. Your own people didn't care enough to come back for you," Wade called over his shoulder. "I suggest you cooperate with the authorities."

Ronnie was still shouting threats and obscenities as Wade secured the packs on the ATV. "Let's go."

Leah paused, folding up the emergency blanket like a pro. "Thanks for the help," she said. "I need to keep going."

"What?" She couldn't be serious. "You need to thaw out and get some real food in your belly," Wade said.

She lifted the GPS unit. "The wolves need me more than I need food. I know where I'm going now."

"I disagree," Wade protested. "My priority is you."

"You found me and helped me a ton already. Thanks."

Exasperated, Wade worked to maintain his

composure. "Let's go back. We can regroup and restock, and make a plan that has a chance of working."

"You're welcome to do all of that." Determination settled across her features. "I've got his pack, the coordinates, and his rifle. I'm going after them."

"You don't even have water. You've been out in the weather too long," Wade said. "It's understandable that you're mad, but you need to take a breath. Think this through."

"I've given this plenty of thought. I know what has to happen. Contrary to what you might believe, I'm perfectly capable."

The whine of another engine approaching startled her into silence. "Get on, now."

"But."

Wade was over the debate. He started the ATV and hauled her on board behind him. "Hang on."

It was a harsh, bumpy ride as he headed east through the trees. The rifle she'd confiscated dug into his back as he took the terrain faster than conditions allowed. He couldn't let Ronnie be found by anyone other than Stone. Couldn't let them learn Leah wasn't dead.

"Is his cell phone on?"

"Yes," she replied. "In the pack."

Good. Hopefully they'd moved away from the scene in time to fool whoever had come back for Ronnie. He kept driving, pushing the vehicle as hard as he could toward the east until a creek forced him north.

He slowed up, listening. Another engine wasn't too far behind them. "His cell is ringing," Leah said.

Wade twisted in his seat. "Toss it into the snow once we're over the rise."

He didn't wait for her agreement, punching the vehicle back into motion.

CHAPTER 3

LEAH GRIPPED the side of the seat tightly, struggling to stay on board and keep the rifle and pack balanced. The wind buffeted her cheeks and she tucked her chin into her collar and scarf, using Wade's broad shoulders as a windbreak. She felt way too exposed without the trees for cover. Sound carried, likely making it easy for whoever was following them. Wade leaned forward, forcing the ATV over the snowy terrain along the creek. More than once, she thought they would wind up in the freezing water, but somehow he muscled the vehicle along a path only he could see.

The tires slipped frequently in the fresh snow, the back end fishtailing as Wade worked to get them up and over the next rise. She started to believe they were making progress solely on his willpower rather than the machine's power.

She peeked over Wade's shoulder, saw that they were nearly over the crest of the hill. When the ATV's front end dipped down, she sent the phone flying, well away from the water. Glancing back, she caught a glimpse of the black device resting on the pristine snow, as if it had simply bounced out of Ronnie's pack at the wrong time.

Now it was a matter of getting away and out of sight before whoever thought they were chasing Ronnie found the phone. Her gaze skimmed the horizon, but there was no obvious escape or place to hide on this side of the creek. They needed a place to stop and cut the engine, otherwise they might as well send up a flare.

Leah fought down the urge to throw herself off the ATV and run for it. She'd never been good at surrendering control. Unfortunately, too many experiences had only reinforced her fear of relying on others. Her inner circle didn't extend far beyond her parents, two close friends she'd known since first grade, and the Guardian Agency. Not that she knew every person they employed, but she'd come to trust their judgment on people.

Apparently, she also trusted Stone Jacobs and the people he chose to work with, since she was letting Wade carry her off on this wild race across Yellowstone.

With her immediate future in Wade's hands, she racked her brain for anything that might help them.

They needed to cross the creek and get out of sight. It was their best hope. Or it would've been if there wasn't a clear trail in the snow behind them.

As if he'd read her mind, Wade tapped her knee, then pointed. Just ahead, the creek narrowed and the rocks on the other side were only dusted with snow. With luck the copse of trees would keep them hidden. Gritting her teeth, she hung on as he maneuvered into the creek. The icy water would be trouble if they had to stay out, unprotected, in the elements much longer. No time to dwell on it as Wade drove up the rocks on the other side and straight for the trees.

In the veil of the trees, she thumped his shoulder and he slowed down. "I'll get the trail," she said, hopping off the ATV.

Grabbing a downed pine bough, she darted back to the creek to brush away the evidence of their route. The world went quiet once more as Wade drove off and cut the engine.

She was at the treeline when she heard the ATV that had been following them. Wade pulled her back into the sparse shadows of the trees, and they dropped to the ground hiding behind the pine needles.

His body pressed against the length of hers, his arm a snug weight as it curled around her midsection. The warmth was welcome, the sensation that someone had her back, even better. Though it was the worst time to feel a spark of attraction, especially for a man she'd just met, she didn't have the energy to fight it. Knowing nothing more would come of this moment and her wayward feelings, she didn't bother blaming it on adrenaline.

The ATV came into view on the other side of the creek. One rider, no helmet, just his hood pulled up over his head. His facial features were hidden by a ski mask and goggles. He slowed down, standing as he drove along the path they'd left behind.

"Ronnie!" he shouted, following the tracks to the place where they'd entered the creek. "Ronnie!"

She took great comfort that the ruse had worked and they'd drawn the rider away from Ronnie's real location.

As Leah and Wade watched, the rider searched for a trail emerging from the creek. The man lifted the radio to his mouth, but she couldn't hear the exchange. He swore and shouted for Ronnie a few more times before finally turning around.

Neither of them moved until the sound faded away.

"Good job," Wade murmured at her ear.

"Same to you," she said. "That was excellent driving."

She should move, had a job to do, but a soft

lethargy had stolen over her senses. She could smell the fresh trees and the crisp snow, and the light exhaust from the ATVs. Through all of that, she caught the masculine scent that was Wade. Bundled up as they were, that shouldn't be possible and yet she knew the fragrance of him was burned into her memory.

Unsettled by the searing awareness, she wriggled away from him and stood up, dusting off the snow. "We need to get moving if we're going to check out the locations Ronnie had saved."

Wade had come to his feet as well and once again she was all too aware of him. He had to be over six feet tall and though it was hard to judge his build precisely due to the necessary outerwear, he carried himself with the confidence and poise of a man who knew his strength and ability.

"Once you're warm again and we're restocked, maybe."

The wolves did not have time for "maybe". She used the GPS unit to figure out the distance to the closest saved point and then searched for any known shelters in between. There was a park ranger station not far off the route, though it was closed for the season. "That makes sense," she said aloud.

"Finally, agreement." Wade smiled down at her, and her belly quivered. "Come on." He touched her elbow lightly, guiding her into the trees.

At the ATV, she picked up the rifle and Ronnie's pack. "You go back to West Yellowstone. I'll find and follow the crew."

"What?" Wade's smile evaporated and a hard scowl shadowed his eyes. "On foot and alone? No way. Your body needs time to warm up," he said.

She shook her head. "This is not a negotiation. I'm not letting them get away with those wolves."

"You can't take them down single handedly."

"Clearly, you don't know me." She took a breath before he could make the suggestion once again. "I've been on this case a long time and this is the closest we've come to solid information on the people involved."

"You have the GPS unit. Stone will soon have Ronnie. We'll come back, fully prepared. I'll bring you myself."

"That's a great offer, but I need to decline."

"Leah, you need to listen."

"Wade, I cannot give up on this. Not when I'm so close." She checked the pack, confirming there was ammunition for the rifle and zipped that pocket closed. "Last year a mother wolf was murdered and her four pups were stolen. Several months later, two separate veterinarians in the Midwest reported juvenile wolves being presented as pets. DNA testing confirmed the animals were gray wolves. This group has run unchecked over this park and the wolf packs for too long. My job--

the job I've trained for--is to get solid intel and break up this crew."

He folded his arms over his chest, his legs braced apart. "My job is to get you back to safety."

"And you did that, thank you." She tried to smile, but it felt brittle on her chapped lips. "Now I'm going. Can I have some water?"

He muttered something unintelligible. She understood why her decision frustrated him, but she wasn't backing down.

He handed her a bottle of water and a couple of energy bars. "This is nonsense. You can't hope to succeed without better supplies and gear."

"Thanks for the assist." Tears stung her nose, but she wouldn't let them fall. "I have a radio. Please let Chelsea know I'll be in touch on the research center channel." With a sniffle, she shrugged into the pack and started off.

Behind her, Wade was talking to someone. They were on a different channel since none of the conversation filtered through her radio. She didn't care. They had separate goals out here and she didn't have enough time to convince him she was right. To go back now would mean losing those wolves.

The pack felt heavy within minutes of setting out. Her feet were still chilled and her lower legs downright cold from the quick run through the creek. Leah didn't dwell on any of it. Her body would warm up with the hike and she could recover once the wolves were safe again.

She focused on moving forward, toward the first location Ronnie had saved. He wasn't the man she'd seen in town, the man who resembled the image in the single grainy photo they had from the hybrid puppy drop off. Having two people connected to the crimes gave her attitude a much-needed boost.

The sound of an ATV startled her and she stumbled over something under the snow. Probably her own feet. On her hands and knees, she braced for trouble, rehearsing the story she had in mind if she got caught. "Out for a hike. ATV died. Going for help." That didn't explain the rifle, but being armed in this vast wilderness wasn't unusual.

"Good grief! Leah!"

Wade's face appeared in front of her. The firm grip on her shoulders felt strange. Maybe she was more exhausted than she realized.

"What are you doing?"

Tears welled in her eyes, blurring her vision. "Hiking."

"Are you crying?"

"It's the wind," she lied, grateful for her sunglasses.

"Good," he said. "I'm no good with tears. Only deal with it during a rescue."

"Lucky you." She shrugged him off. Pushed to her feet. "Have a good day."

"Come with me, Leah. You're in no condition to help those wolves."

"Have to." She took a few more shaky steps. Blinked until her vision was clear. "Bye."

"No one mentioned I'd be rescuing a crazy person," he muttered.

"I heard that."

"Good." Somehow his hand had slipped around her waist and she was on her feet, being led to the ATV.

He sat her down while he relieved her of the pack and rifle. His hands were so gentle, his movements efficient. Easy to believe those hands had rescued loads of people in worse shape than she was. Then she felt abruptly alone as he secured the gear on the back of the vehicle.

She should say thank you. Had she thanked him earlier? The words were sluggish as she forced them past her lips. "Thanks, W-wade."

"No problem." He climbed in front of her. Before he started driving, he took her hands and put them on his coat. "Can you hang on?"

She nodded. "Y-yes," she managed. "Not town. Please."

"No. Trust me, Leah."

"All right." She didn't have a choice. Her brain

might as well be wrapped in cotton, she felt so foggy and detached. Exhaustion and exposure could do that. It required all of her concentration just to grip his coat as the ATV started forward.

She wanted to keep track of where they were going, but her eyelids kept drooping. Her head bounced off Wade's shoulder at least twice as he drove along until she couldn't fight it any longer.

WADE HAD NEVER BEEN MORE grateful to find a roadway. It had been plowed recently enough that he could see the pavement most of the time. Pushing the vehicle as hard as he dared, he raced toward the ranger station that kept them closest to the saved point on Ronnie's GPS.

Through the years, he and the team had made plenty of rescues without the benefit of clear roads or paths. Succeeding despite a lack of normal access was their specialty. This situation was different. The significance of Leah's rescue weighed on him, though he couldn't pin down why.

He didn't know Leah, couldn't claim any deep understanding of her, but he could definitely relate to her iron-clad determination to complete the assignment. When she woke, he hoped to clarify that his goal wasn't to hold her back. He was applying every facet of his skillset to keep her safe enough to succeed.

Her body had succumbed to her ordeal long before the ranger station came into view. She slumped against his back, her grip slack. Trained or not, eventually the body trumped willpower and intent, shutting down when it had enough.

Wade breathed easier when they reached the ranger station. The modest single-story stone and log cottage looked like a fortress against the backdrop of a big sky, mountain peaks and the snowy landscape. Even better, as he cut the ATV engine, he heard the sound of a helicopter rotor. Supplies were almost here.

It meant the world to him that he could always count on Justice.

It was nice to have a direct link to the park ranger service too. As a group, Team Wolf coordinated with local law enforcement and first responders whenever they came in for a consult or assist. Coming to Yellowstone was no different. Eris Lange, a local park ranger and now extended family since pairing up with Alex, had given him the code for the door.

Parking the ATV as close to the front door as possible, he carefully shifted around so Leah wouldn't fall. With a little luck, he might get her inside before she realized what was happening.

Cradling her shoulders, he slipped an arm

under her knees and scooped up her slender body, holding her snug against his chest. She came around, her eyelids fluttering, and then tucked her head under his chin, out like a light.

He managed to enter the code and open the door while holding her and stepped into the dim light of the cabin. The inside was almost as cold as outside, but being out of the wind was a big relief. He closed the door with his foot, then got Leah settled on a couch near the fireplace. He threw his coat over her while he searched for bedding. Finding the right storage closet, he chose several thick blankets and tucked them around her.

Wade quickly got a fire going with the kindling and firewood left on the stone hearth. Once the blaze was pumping out heat, he unloaded the ATV, storing everything in the small utility room off the kitchen so he could sort things without waking Leah.

Taking an instant hot pack out of the emergency kit, he returned to her and moved the blankets just enough to get her out of her boots and socks. Kneeling on the floor, he rested the hot pack between her ankles, using the fabric of her pants to protect her skin. He was tucking the multiple layers around her feet again to seal in the warmth when the front door opened.

Wade turned as Justice walked in, his arms full of a large box and a bag slung across his body to rest at his hip. He placed the items near the door before hauling Wade up and into a bone-crushing hug. "I was worried, man."

"You must be if you left the helo all alone," Wade said when they stepped apart.

Justice grinned. "Payton's chopper-sitting for me."

"Still using that sexy pilot angle, huh?" Wade teased.

"Why mess with perfection?" His grin faded as he looked around, his gaze lingering on Leah. "What angle are you working here?"

"The angle that keeps her alive," Wade replied. He tipped his head, leading Justice toward the kitchen. His voice low, he gave Justice a quick rundown of events since finding Leah this morning.

His brother had several questions relevant to the current crises and the discussion helped Wade reclaim his perspective. "As for good news, Stone picked up the guy you left in the woods. Delivered him to the sheriff personally."

"That's great news." Wade pushed a hand through his hair. He would've been furious if their risky ride had been for nothing. "Maybe he'll roll on his crew."

"We can hope." Justice bumped his knuckles in a quick rhythm on the countertop. "All of the surrounding airfields are on alert," he added. "What are you going to do now?"

"Help her," he replied. "That's what we do."

"Right." Justice cocked his head. "Any chance you'll let me airlift the two of you out of here?"

It was the smart move, but he couldn't do that to Leah. "No, but I appreciate the offer."

"You should." His grin flashed and faded. "Any idea how you'll proceed from here? There's just two of you and the crew is probably long gone with those wolves by now."

His brother was right and he knew it. "She and I will talk after we rest and regroup. No way she'll give up the chase if there's any hope of gaining real intel on these guys." He didn't have to know Leah well to recognize her dogged determination to get something positive out of this nightmare.

"All right," Justice said, clearly resigned. "I brought food, dry clothes for both of you, and the usual essentials."

Wade smiled, knowing that phrase covered a wealth of useful items. "Thanks, we'll make the most of it."

"You do that. Keep us in the loop. We're all here, all ready to jump in if you need us. One more thing. What should I tell Mom?"

Justice wasn't Marie Fielding's biological son, but no one would know it. Since the day Justice had walked into her kitchen with Wade, he'd become her son in all the ways that mattered. Up to and including the occasional sibling rivalry.

"Since when do you tell her anything about an op?"

"An op." Justice snorted and bobbed his eyebrows up and down. "You were on your knees in front of Leah. Mom shouldn't be the last to know if you're about to propose."

Wade gave him a shove. His brother was a menace and way too cocky about romantic relationships since falling in love with Payton. "There's nothing to know. Get going." Justice yanked him close and slapped his back. "Whatever you say." He darted out of reach and left the cabin through the back door, preserving the heat in the front room. Wade stared out at the horizon, lost in his own thoughts, until the steady thump of the helicopter's rotors faded away.

He plugged in the coffee maker and brewed a pot of coffee. Filling a thick ceramic mug, he sipped immediately, savoring the heat and flavor. For a few minutes, he stared out through the kitchen window at the snowy landscape, considering the options.

He'd rescued Leah from almost certain frost-bite, hypothermia, and possibly worse. They were safe here. For now. But as he'd told Justice, she wouldn't turn back, not when she had a chance to make a difference.

He went out to the front room to check on her. She was sound asleep, her breathing deep and even. One gloved hand was tucked under her chin. Her forehead still felt too cool under his fingertips. He threw another log on the fire, watched it catch, and then went back to the bigger bedroom, taking the quilt off the bed.

Leah's only reaction was to nestle deeper under the multiple layers.

Needing to stay busy and keep himself warm, he hauled the supplies Justice had delivered to the kitchen. He unpacked the various items, storing the food and taking the clothing to the bedrooms. In the bag he found a rugged laptop and a card with the WiFi access code the park rangers used.

Having done as much as possible for Leah, he refilled his coffee mug and headed for the bathroom to shower. He considered it one more facet of care that he took the ATV keys and her boots along with him.

He shouldn't have worried about her running off and continuing the chase without him. She slept through his shower, slept through his rattling around in the kitchen as he prepared hot soup and cheese sandwiches.

After he ate his fill, he took the laptop and settled in the chair near the fire to keep an eye on Leah. He propped his feet on the hearth and logged on to research the exotic pets and hybrid wolves issues. Though he was tempted to snoop around for some background on Leah, he resisted the temptation.

A few hours later, it was dark outside and he had an uncomfortable new awareness about the crimes she was so desperate to stop. The wolves had enough trouble surviving without the off-kilter people cherry-picking their packs and using the animals for financial gain or hybrid breeding.

Like it or not, she wasn't alone in the hunt any longer. Wade would be her partner until they recovered those wolves.

He dragged himself away from the welcome comfort of the fire and went to the kitchen to call Stone. "Get anything out of Ronnie?" he asked as soon as his new boss picked up. It would be a big boost if he could give Leah hard intel when she came around.

"Claims he's just a cog in the wheel," Stone said. "He copped to taking shots at the helicopter, denied that he was there to kill Leah or anyone else."

"Leah didn't make that up," Wade said. "I saw his face."

"Take it easy. I'm on your side," Stone reminded him. "And we're all aware he's lying."

"I've kept the radio on, but there's only silence on the channel they were using."

"The team is working on it here. We'll let you know as soon as we hear any relevant chatter."

Wade appreciated the support and the assurance. "They can't walk out of the park with those wolves, especially not down a man." They'd ambushed the pack, and moved east through the trees. They were using an ATV out here and those were illegal aside from official use. Which left Wade wondering if that first location was a rendezvous with a better vehicle. Maybe more than one, considering they had to load an ATV and hide the wolves.

"Want me to send up Justice again tomorrow?"

"Please. I think that's a must," Wade said. "Have him search the closest roads and intersections east of where Leah was found."

"I can do that."

"As soon as Leah is rested, I'll take her to the locations saved on Ronnie's GPS device." Wade didn't worry about pushing her too hard or fast. The bigger challenge would be convincing her to give herself time to recover. "Justice brought what we'll need to keep going."

"Sounds like a plan. Remember you have our full support," Stone said.

The call ended and Wade was restless. He wished Justice had delivered some beer. Or a bottle of whiskey. Something stronger than coffee and hot chocolate. The alcohol might help, but nothing could erase the appalling articles and dreadful photographs of the exotic pet trade he'd found online. All of it was seared into his memory now.

Wade eyed the gear scattered on the countertop in the utility room and picked up the GPS unit. Back in front of the fire, he entered the coordinates for both locations on the laptop. The larger screen allowed him a more thorough study of the terrain around each area.

Using the software, he added the location where he'd found Leah and the point where the wolves had been ambushed. He was deep in thought when Leah stirred, the blankets shifting as she stretched. She swiped at the hair that fell into her face, then frowned at her glove-covered hand.

He watched, curious and wary about her reaction. Her big brown eyes scanned the ceiling, then locked with his. "Wade?"

"The same. How are you feeling?"

She struggled with her gloves. "I don't know yet."

He set aside the laptop and crouched in front of her, taking her gloves off one at a time, putting the pair next to her boots on the hearth. "Plenty of time to decide." He helped her shake off the blankets, watching for any shivering or other signs of distress.

"What did you do?" she asked, her gaze landing on the heat pack as it slipped to the floor. She wiggled her bare toes, then jerked a blanket over her feet. "Where are we?"

"In order, I found shelter. We both needed it. We're at a ranger station. Alone." Anticipating her next question, he added, "A station closer to that first location on Ronnie's GPS unit."

Her entire body relaxed, relief washed over her face, softening her features. "Thank you."

"Ready for a tour?" He held out a hand.

She set her hand in his, letting him help her to her feet. The contact sizzled through him, more potent than the whiskey he'd been wishing for earlier.

"As long as you start with the bathroom."

Her candid request cut through the physical distraction and he forced a light laugh as he led the way. "Shower is stocked and those are clean towels for you on the counter." He pointed to the stack. "You'll find clean, dry clothes in the front bedroom when you're ready."

"Wow. Thanks, Wade."

She closed the door in his face and he turned away, headed for the kitchen to reheat the soup and make a sandwich for her. As far as he could tell, sleep and warmth had been exactly what she'd needed. Her skin had some color again and she'd been steady on her feet.

Her bare feet.

Another image he wouldn't soon forget. Didn't

want to. Normally, he didn't find feet all that sexy. They were necessary, obviously. Sometimes ticklish, but not exactly at the top of the list of hot turn-ons. Earlier, taking off her socks, he hadn't really noticed. Because in that instance she'd felt more like a victim rescued, in need of his professional expertise and assistance.

Now, awake and refreshed, she had an undeniable presence that roused his senses and his curiosity. Self-discipline kept him in the kitchen when he heard the shower taps turn off, followed by the squeaky hinge of the bathroom door. He poured a glass of water for her and set it on the table. She would need to hydrate after the weather, stress, and hours of sleep. He quickly dismissed the idea of bringing in the laptop. She needed some time to focus on herself and her wellbeing before they made plans.

The skillet was hot and the soup bubbling when Leah joined him in the kitchen. "Better?" he asked.

"Much."

He turned to ask about her sandwich preferences and lost his train of thought. Her long dark hair had been woven into a loose braid that curved around her neck and down over one shoulder. She wore dark yoga pants and a long-sleeved cream-colored thermal shirt under a flannel she'd left unbuttoned. She rolled the sleeves back as he watched. Thick socks covered her feet.

Mentally, he cursed Justice for planting relationship thoughts in his head. Leah was a victim, basically, and he needed to view her in that context. They weren't here on a romantic getaway, they were here as a matter of survival. He was sure she'd want to continue her hunt for the wolves and it would be easier to help her if his focus was clear.

"Who do I thank for the wardrobe?" Finished with the sleeves, she looked up and met his gaze.

Her big eyes, the easy and friendly expression framed by thick dark eyelashes, hit him with all the force of a mule-kick to the chest. His breath stalled and he rubbed a hand over his sternum. "Oh. Um. That would be my brother, Justice Kane. Likely with help or guidance from Chelsea or Payton. You want a grilled ham and cheese to go with the soup?"

Her stomach rumbled and her lips curled up in a sheepish smile. "Guess that's a yes."

"I'll make it quick," he promised. "Have a seat, start hydrating."

"Yes, sir," she said in a breezy tone. "Did you mean Payton Wheeler?"

"That's right." He got the sandwich made and set it to cook in the skillet. "You know her?"

"Only by name. Cursory background stuff. The research center has a list of ranches in the vicinity."

He shot her a look. It was good as a cover line,

delivered smoothly. What would it take for her to open up about her real employer?

She shrugged and drank more water. "Research is an essential part of my job."

"And your job is breaking up this exotic pet ring."

"It is today," she stated. "Guess you've done some digging too."

"Not into you." He flipped the sandwich to brown the other side. "Just the issue at large."

"Come up with any insightful conclusions?"

He judged he had a minute or two on the sandwich and moved to refill her water. "Why aren't you yelling at me that we need to get moving to save the wolves?"

Her dark eyebrows arched and the spark in her eyes was mesmerizing. "I'm resigned to my fate?"

"Not buying it." Not after the way she argued so passionately to keep pressing on.

Her smile washed over him like the hot water in the shower earlier. Warm, sweet, and oh, so welcome.

"Fair enough. Apparently, I'm much more personable and reasonable when I'm not half frozen. I'm frustrated for sure and antsy about the wolves, but you obviously took great care with me, Wade. I appreciate that." Her mouth softened. "Besides, it's dark out, we have the GPS unit, and

I'm about to enjoy a fabulous meal. If you don't burn it."

He spun back to the skillet, sliding the sandwich from skillet to plate in the nick of time. "Crust or no crust?"

Only one eyebrow lifted this time. "I'm not a child."

Chuckling, he cut the sandwich in half, ladled soup into a bowl and brought it all to the table for her. She closed her eyes and inhaled deeply. "Smells so good."

"Dig in." Was she always so sensual when she wasn't half-frozen and chasing bad guys? He kept the question locked down for a more appropriate time. Somewhere around never.

"You're not eating?" she asked after a few minutes.

"I chowed down earlier," he replied. "There's plenty more when you're ready."

"Your brother, I presume?"

He nodded. "He's got a gift for supplies." Unsure what to do with himself, Wade poured another cup of coffee.

"How are you related?" she asked. "Your last names are different," she added when he only stared at him.

She was studying him with a curious intensity. He couldn't decide if it was amusing or irritating. At the very least it put them on even ground since he was curious about her too. "True. We were best friends. As far back as I can remember. Now we're brothers. The lack of DNA didn't get in the way of us becoming family."

"That's good." She returned to her meal, eventually requesting a refill on the soup and the water. He was beyond grateful she wasn't arguing about taking the time to recuperate.

She finished her meal and carried her dishes to the sink. He would've happily handled the chore himself, but she insisted. "You cooked," she said. "I'll clean." She ran hot water into the sink, added dish soap. "We should talk about tomorrow," she said as she worked.

He grabbed a dish towel. She couldn't expect him to just sit and watch her handle the chore alone. Not after what she'd been through. "I pinned the known locations into a map while I was researching."

"Researching," she echoed. Her hands went still in the soapy water. "Me or the situation?"

"Situation," he replied, pleased that he could be one hundred percent honest about that. What was she so afraid he might learn about her? Her concern seemed to run deeper than an employer issue. "I think you'll be pleased we're starting from here tomorrow," he said, keeping his voice neutral.

Her dark eyes blazed with anticipation. Time and again, he was amazed how much a person could change after a few hours of rest. Seeing Leah like this, it was easy to understand why the people who knew her had been adamant about her integrity and her will to survive.

He suspected the two of them would need both of those character traits in spades to save those wolves.

CHAPTER 4

IN THE MAIN ROOM, Leah sat on the floor, a blanket on her lap and her back to the warmth of the fire. Wade pulled the coffee table close and set up the laptop, pulling up the map he'd been working with. He sat down next to her, his knee bumping against hers and his body heat nearly as warm as the flames in the hearth.

His clean, masculine scent wafted over her and she had to work not to lean in closer. It seemed as if he radiated safety and confidence. Growing up the daughter of a professor and a veterinarian, she'd met people from all over the world. Her latest career move had expanded that circle even more. During her recent assignment with the rodeo crowd she'd watched outrageous bravado, friendly flirtation, and off-the-chart risk taking. None of it appealed to her as much as Wade's steadiness.

She wondered if Wade had always been this way or if his calm, self-assured presence had been cultivated by his years of service?

The question was irrelevant. They were out here with a job to do. And they were right here, side by side, to make a solid action plan.

"These are the locations we know," he said. "Where the pack was ambushed, along with the saved points from the GPS."

"You're right," she murmured, studying the display. "We're actually at an advantage starting from here in the morning. We have much more manageable terrain coming at the lodge from this side."

Wade tilted his head. "Assuming that point is their next stop. It could be the place where they waited for location intel on the pack."

"I don't think so," she mused. "That lodge closed for the season last month. The hybrid wolf-dogs showed up at vet offices six months ago. Factoring breeding and other factors, this can't be a pre-ambush spot. Why would the gang risk being recognized by staying at the lodge when it's open?"

"You make a good point."

She didn't hear any sarcasm in his voice, only respect. It made her want to share more about herself, and what brought her here. Worse, she felt the urge to get personal. Not the time for that. She needed to focus. Those wolves were counting on her. The Guardian Agency was counting on her to find a workable lead.

"Either we find the gang and the wolves or, if they've moved on, we search for clues or evidence. Can your group find out if the lodge has any kind of security system?"

Wade pulled out his phone and sent a text. "We can try."

She wanted to ask her research assistant to jump on this as well, but her phone was long gone. "If I can borrow your phone, I can ask a computer-geek friend to search too."

To her relief he didn't balk at the request or brag about the Brotherhood Protectors's resources. He handed her the device and leaned back on his hands, his gaze on the map. She sent her message to the number she'd memorized and placed the phone on the table.

He sighed. "It'll be hard going without a clear road. Harder still between the close point and the one to the northwest."

"For us and them," she pointed out. "We know they have at least one ATV, since it chased us. Logic dictates they're using a bigger vehicle to move the wolves they captured."

"That doesn't necessarily make it easier after fresh snowfall."

"You think we can find the truck?"

He turned the full force of his attention on her.

She was grateful to be sitting down as her knees turned watery and a delicious shiver rolled through her. "You're cold again." He reached out and rubbed her shoulders, nudging her closer to the fire. "Let me build it up."

"No." She sputtered out a husky, nervous laugh. "No, I'm fine. We need to plan."

He sat back down, his gaze intent and sincere. She felt utterly caught and thoroughly excited. "We leave at first light for the closed lodge. With luck, we'll find something useful to take to the authorities."

And there it was again. One more excellent opening to come clean about her intentions. "Even better if we find the gang with the wolves. We need to reunite those wolves with their pack."

Wade stood up. "I'll get the gear together," he said. "You stay here and keep warm. Then we'll get to bed."

Her cheeks flamed as her imagination got stuck on those last words. Fortunately, he walked off, apparently oblivious. Sharing a bed with Wade was bound to be a memorable experience. Again, irrelevant and inappropriate. A sweet, safe fantasy to indulge in later. Much later, when this was all over and she was off on a new case.

She returned her attention to the map. "Where are you hiding?" she murmured. It didn't make sense, outside of the GPS information, that they would be moving the wolves east. It kept the wolves and the gang on protected land, remote as it was. Yet they'd acted with absolute confidence that they could get away with it. They hadn't tried to run her off last night, they'd gone straight to attempted murder.

Scooting closer to the laptop, she opened a new tab and logged into her email to send a detailed update to her research assistant. She included the unfortunate news that her cell phone was a casualty of the attack last night as well as the information from the GPS device.

She finished the message with the warning that she would probably be out of contact for the next few days.

She signed out and closed the window just as Wade's phone flashed with an incoming call. Popping to her feet, she grabbed the phone and hustled toward the kitchen.

Wade must have heard the ring tone as he was rushing toward her. They collided in the doorway. He caught her arms, keeping her steady. His grip was strong, and gentle. A pleasant, completely different heat sizzled through her system.

"Stone," he said. "Calling to make sure you're still alive, no doubt."

"What? Oh. Right." She'd forgotten all about the phone in her hands, thoroughly distracted by the man in front of her. "Here."

She retreated to the other room as he answered the call. She really needed to pull herself together. These off-kilter reactions had to be fallout from the exhaustion, exposure, and pure adrenaline she'd been running on for too long.

And come tomorrow, there would be more of the same, assuming they caught up with the gang and the wolves they'd stolen. She paced in front of the fire working through the various threats and problems ahead.

"Leah?" Wade was watching her from the doorway. "Stone wants to speak with you."

That seemed wildly out of character. She'd never had reason to speak with Stone Jacobs in the past. Cautiously, she crossed the room and took the phone as if it might explode at any moment. "Hello?"

"Ms. Williams, Stone Jacobs. Patrick Gamble and Hank Patterson have just read-in Wade and I on the full scope of your assignment in Yellowstone. You can consider this a joint operation moving forward."

She glanced over her shoulder at Wade. It wasn't much of a stretch to trust the man who'd rescued her and helped her escape the gang's pursuit. But there were protocols to follow and she didn't want to be maneuvered into a partnership. How could she be sure Wade would be as dedicated to the wolf rescue as she was?

"I'll need confirmation from my own team," she said.

"Gamble anticipated that," Stone said. "Hold on."

A moment later, Gamble's voice greeted her. "Are you okay, Leah?"

"Yes, thank you, sir."

"You can pull back," he said. "Take some time to rest while research digs into this."

She rolled her shoulders back, her jaw tight. "I don't think that's the best course of action." They'd trained her to speak her mind, valuing intuition as well as verified facts. "Last night was a rough one, but I'm fine now."

"Thanks to Mr. Fielding."

"In part, yes." More than part, but she needed her boss to focus on the wolves. "We have more intel now." She paused, took a breath. "One member of the ambush team is in the sheriff's custody already."

"I heard," Gamble confirmed. "Are you comfortable with Mr. Fielding?"

"Yes." She'd wanted to do this on her own, had been prepared to finish this as a solo act, but having Wade along increased her odds exponentially. If he was committed to the cause. "We have a plan," she continued calmly. "And I believe we've found our best lead on the breeding site so far."

"All right. I understand your investment in this

case, Leah. I've vetted Mr. Fielding and I'm confident the two of you will work well together."

"Yes, sir."

"Stone tells me there's no easy way to replace your phone," Gamble said.

"He's not wrong." It was hard to explain just how wild and remote Yellowstone really was. Looking at a map didn't clarify things much. The rugged, gorgeous landscape hadn't been tamed, not even in the twenty-first century, and current conveniences couldn't be taken for granted.

"That's fine," Gamble said. "I'll give this number to your research assistant so you can be in contact."

"All right." She would just have to be okay with Wade seeing her messages. Wasn't like she'd be hiding much now. "We'll send information as soon as it's available."

When Gamble ended the call, Leah gazed into the fire, her hands clutching Wade's phone.

"Please don't toss it in," he said from behind her.

She whirled around and found herself way too close. Her heart thundered and she blamed it on surprise rather than his proximity. "Pardon?"

He took the phone out of her hands, dropping it into a pocket. "Looked like you were about to throw it into the fire."

"No." She pushed her hands into her hair. "No. I wouldn't do that. Sorry."

"For what?"

"I'm not exactly comfortable with a partner," she declared. A research assistant watching her back was one thing. Teamwork had never been her strong suit. Solo assignments in the Guardian Agency were one of the big perks in her opinion.

"Why not?"

She was not dredging up all the answers to that question. "An only child thing, I guess."

"Ah." He rocked back on his heels. "I always thought being an only child would be cool."

She chuckled. "And I always wanted siblings." Folding her arms, she studied him. The man had questions in those warm eyes. Reclaiming the blanket, she tucked herself into the end of the couch, feet curled under her. "Ask away."

He cocked his head. "What do you mean?"

"My boss shared why he sent me to West Yellowstone, but I'm sure you have more questions."

"They said you're out here tracking down some illegal wolf-dog breeder." Wade perched on the edge of a chair, elbows braced on his thighs. "What did you see that made you ignore the incoming weather?"

"Oh." It wasn't the question she was expecting. And he didn't seem to be judging her decision, even if it had resulted in a situation that dragged him into her crisis. "I volunteered to go take a look when the drone flight noticed trouble. And I was furious when I saw the wolf that had been shot. Still am." She deliberately relaxed her hands when her fingers curled into fists. "I documented the scene and would've come back..." Her voice trailed off.

"Except?"

"Tranq darts were left behind." She struggled to speak without anger. "The trail of dragging wolves away was clear." She lifted her eyes, meeting his gaze. "And I thought I recognized a new face in town last week. A man bearing a strong resemblance to an image we have around the time of a hybrid delivery."

Wade made a low whistle. "That's serious."

"Only if I'm right. It wasn't Ronnie. This guy is younger, lanky. I couldn't find out anything about him before the ambush on the pack, but I just cannot believe it was a coincidence."

"That makes sense." Wade slid back in the chair. "Did you tell anyone?"

"Not in town. No one knew about my real assignment. I couldn't get close enough to get a picture with my phone without getting caught. I sent the information to my research assistant, but she couldn't find a good image of him on any security cameras around town."

"Does West Yellowstone even have a traffic camera?"

"There's a camera at the park entrance, that's

about it. So far, the guy I believe is connected didn't enter the park at that point."

"And you didn't see him specifically at the ambush site."

"No."

Wade nodded, but he had to be thinking she'd imagined any resemblance.

"Look, I realize how it sounds."

"Do you?"

She reined in her flash of temper and shifted the subject. "This breeding operation is dangerous. There is absolutely no reason to create a hybrid wolf-dog. We don't have any work for them. Wolves as pets are a bad idea all around. Hybrids aren't any better."

Wade held up his hands in surrender. "I'm not arguing, Leah. You sound like an expert."

"On this case, I am." She didn't want to get into the rest of her sordid history with vet school or how she'd wound up with the Guardian Agency. "I'm intent on this, but I'm trained. Focused and determined, but I'm not out of control."

"I never said you were."

"Come on. You must be thinking it, considering I chose pursuit over a clear weather risk."

He leaned forward once more. "How about we make a deal right now? I won't tell you what you're thinking and you do me the same courtesy."

A weight lifted from her shoulders. If he meant

it, if he kept to that deal, this unexpected partnership might work out after all. "All right."

"I don't know the Guardian Agency, but I know Stone. And Hank. They don't work with subpar talent." He gave her a wide, charming smile that sent a jolt of heat through her system. "I'm proof of that."

"Fair point," she allowed.

His smile softened and his earnest gaze soothed her frayed nerves. "You have my word, I'll do everything possible to help you find the wolves and the men who took them."

"I believe you." She took a shaky breath. "Thank you. This is as close as we've come to making a dent in the operation."

"Then we should both get some rest. Tomorrow, we'll see if we can crack it open and put it out of commission forever."

"I'm all for that," she said.

Wade banked the fire and within the hour, they had a departure time and route planned. After checking the packs and supplies, she went to the bedroom and slid under the covers. Grateful for the thick blankets and cozy quilt, she tried to quiet her mind.

It wasn't easy. After nearly a year of watching and waiting, the illegal breeders were almost within her grasp. The biggest assignment of her career might be solved as early as tomorrow. To make that happen, she needed to be well-rested, recharged, and ready for anything.

Closing her eyes, she thought of how good it would feel when this gang was in custody, answering for their many crimes. She wasn't sure when her thoughts drifted to Wade and his calm presence, his steady gaze, and his sexy mouth, but she enjoyed the hot dreams that followed.

IN THE NEXT BEDROOM, Wade tossed and turned in the dark. He checked his phone and confirmed he was awake a full hour ahead of the alarm he'd set. Flopping back on the pillow, he resigned himself to the sexy dream that had brought him out of a deep sleep.

Leah had been in his arms, her body poised over his, her silky hair caressing his chest.

If only.

He blamed the occurrence on basic physiology and proximity. The woman had been pressed against him on the ATV, giving him a tantalizing understanding of her lovely body. Sex dreams happened. The attraction wasn't a surprise. Leah was stunningly beautiful. But her appeal didn't mean anything. Couldn't. Not out here when they had a job to do. She'd had no choice but to trust him when she was vulnerable. He wouldn't break that trust by making a move on her while they were working.

Normally, he'd get up and get moving anyway. No sense wasting energy or time.

But doing that might wake Leah and she needed every minute of recovery she could get.

As partners went, she wasn't exactly his ideal. Too many unknowns and, yes, he had a few concerns about her judgment when it came to the wolves.

For Wade, human welfare always came first. The wolves were essential for the ecosystem, he understood that. They were powerful, smart apex predators who kept things balanced in the food chain.

He admired the dedication that brought Leah out into the danger zone and her determination to stop the criminal activity. But she wasn't running at one-hundred percent. Given a choice, Wade would keep her away from the front lines, give her more time to recuperate.

He nearly laughed, thinking of how vehemently she'd protest if he made such a suggestion.

This wasn't the military and she'd been working this case a whole lot longer than he had. She had plenty of grit to go with her wilderness survival skills. He respected her drive, having pushed himself to the limit on various assignments. It was more than a little comforting that both his boss and hers had given him the authority to call off the search if it posed an unreasonable physical threat.

Another pesky detail he would keep to himself. With luck, she'd never have to know.

He checked the current weather report on his phone, fully aware things could change. They'd packed accordingly, from supplies to weapons, and were as prepared as they could be.

Whatever they did or didn't find today at the nearest GPS point Ronnie had saved, Wade would protect Leah first and foremost. Justice had included a couple of tracking tags he could use if he was forced to choose between her safety and the safety of the wolves.

It was obvious her focus would be on saving the animals and she needed someone watching her back, guarding her from the gang that wanted her dead.

That singular fact worried him more than a little. To have the gang leap to such extreme ruthless action didn't bode well for an easy takedown.

Good thing he enjoyed a challenge.

CHAPTER 5

DAWN WAS a golden wisp of light on the horizon as Leah and Wade loaded the ATV. Breakfast had been a relatively quiet affair. Neither of them seemed to be in the mood for chatter as they gulped coffee and fueled up on eggs, sausage, and toast.

Outside, they found a clear and cold morning and the easterly wind racing over the open terrain promised to make the ride ahead of them even more challenging.

Wade straddled the ATV, leaning forward to give Leah room to settle behind him. She paused first to adjust the balaclava so it covered more of his face. "That wind will rip right through you otherwise."

She couldn't see his mouth, only the smile flickering in his gaze. "Thanks," he said, reaching to snap the flap of her coat to cover her neck. He pulled sunglasses down over his eyes, waiting for her to do the same. "Now we're ready."

She gave him a quick nod and climbed into her seat. As Wade drove, she watched the first rays of sunlight dance across the fresh snow. Mornings like this made it easy to believe they were the only people in the world.

But they weren't. Somewhere out here Ronnie's pals were escaping with several wild wolves. She couldn't stop wondering how much progress they'd made overnight.

While Wade drove toward the closed campground, she scanned the horizon for any sign of the thieves. After yesterday's chase, they knew the gang had at least one ATV in addition to a vehicle big enough to haul the wolves. The expansive park seemed daunting, even knowing where the gang was likely headed. Thick wooded areas and vast snow-covered meadows would pose challenges for any vehicle.

Their persistence was their only advantage and they needed to make the most of it.

After a couple of hours, Wade stopped for a water break.

"Do you think the roadblocks will be set in time?" she wondered.

"I'm sure of it." Wade took a long drink and wiped his mouth. "Reduces their options."

"Plenty of unmarked ways out, though."

"True," he allowed. "We have to think positively." He frowned as he gazed out over the terrain. "Did you hear any kind of engine nearby when you gave chase?"

"No. It was quiet. They must've dragged the wolves a long way before moving out."

"All right. Let's keep moving."

A few minutes later, Wade pulled to a stop close to another wooded area. "Thought I saw a reflection. Sunlight off glass," he said. "And nowhere near a paved road."

Excitement surged through her. She didn't think either of them took a breath while they listened. His eyes flashed with triumph when the sound of an engine drifted their way.

Wade pushed the ATV to the limit, trying to get close enough for a visual.

Soon it was evident they were closing in on someone who didn't care about leaving a trail. There were broken branches and tire treads visible in the snow.

"Moving straight for the campground," Leah said when Wade paused again. "With all the stealth of a bull in a china shop."

"Impatience will kill you. Something my mom said when I started driving," Wade explained. "Even more applicable out here." He looked around. "They're too confident, despite losing contact with Ronnie."

A metallic clang echoed nearby and Wade immediately moved the ATV closer to the trees and out of sight. Leah hopped off and darted toward the sound.

Wade caught her sleeve. "Slowly," he warned, touching his lips with a gloved finger.

She nodded, taking a breath and slowing down. The sounds continued, reminding her of the metal holding cages at her mother's vet practice.

"Hurry up," someone shouted from just out of sight.

More clanging followed, along with indistinguishable voices.

Wade tapped her shoulder and used hand signals that she assumed were from his Army days. Not knowing what the signals meant, she obeyed common sense, ducking down and staying low as she moved forward.

She didn't hear Wade move, but glancing back, she saw he was several yards away. The guy was scary good. She had a feeling she was going to need that kind of skill set on her side in order to rescue those wolves and bring down the illegal breeder.

WITH HIS EYES ON LEAH, Wade paused just long enough to send their coordinates back to head-quarters. He didn't wait to see if the message went through. Leah was hell-bent on recovering those wolves. Even though she ultimately wanted the breeder, he knew she'd be tempted to save the wolves if she had the chance.

Couldn't blame her.

He agreed with Chelsea's assessment that Leah was the genuine article. She was clearly passionate about wolf welfare and conservation. He'd find the qualities more appealing if they weren't navigating a tightrope with life or death hanging in the balance.

Sure would be nice if he could get a second opinion from Justice. Although Wade trusted his own instincts, he'd stumbled into a complicated situation. Being attracted didn't help. Working search and rescue, it was imperative to have confidence in addition to a realistic self-assessment. He'd taken on a basic search and rescue op and landed in the wilderness with a woman who was sitting on the cusp of something huge.

As he took in the scene in the clearing, it gave him chills that she'd planned to handle this on her own.

An older model gray pickup truck sat in a clearing in front of a weather-beaten cabin. The bed was weighed down with four heavy-duty cages and each cage held a quiet, wary wolf. An ATV was a few yards away. Two men worked near the back of the truck, while a third filled the ATV's gas tank.

"What the hell is the problem?" the first man demanded as he capped the gas can.

"Ease up, Chuck," a man near the tailgate shot back. "You want to lose the cargo?" He unwound a roll of brand-new strapping. "Catch!"

The lanky man on the far side of the truck missed and laughed it off. "You throw like a girl, Denny."

"I shoot like a man," Denny countered, his voice low. "Come on. Strap it down before he blows a gasket."

The two men worked swiftly securing the cages, giving the captured wolves plenty of space. Chuck stalked in and out of the cabin while Denny moved toward the ATV and pulled on some gloves. The third man pulled out his phone and held it up high, the wolves in the background.

"What the hell are you doing now, Tyson?" Chuck asked as he headed for the driver's side.

"Selfies," Tyson responded. "And proof of life."

Chuck swore. "Just get in the damn truck."

"Yes, sir." He paused to test that the heavy padlocks on each of the crates was secure.

Wade caught movement on the far side of the cabin. Leah. She was well-hidden from the men and Wade suspected she was preparing to shoot. Time to improvise.

Denny straddled the ATV. "Ready when… Hey, who the hell are you?"

He dropped his handgun, keeping only his pack, and pulled his mask up over his face.

"Hey, man! I thought I was alone out here," Wade said, channeling his best friendly hiker impression. "Whoa, dude are those wolves?"

Tyson hustled forward and Chuck moved to flank him, his gaze raking the area. All Wade could do was hope Leah kept her head.

"You first," Chuck said. "Who are you?"

"Clint Bromley." Wade stuck out his hand. None of the men moved close enough to shake his hand. "Is this your place?"

"Alone isn't a thing you should be in Yellowstone, man," Tyson said.

Wade tried to peek around the men to see the wolves. "They look wild. I can't believe I'm this close."

"Too close." Chuck closed in. "You need to go."

"Now," Denny added.

"The guides say that wolves avoid people," Wade rambled, angling to get a look at the tailgate. All the other men kept shifting to block his view.

He didn't dare glance Leah's way.

"Keep your eyes open," Chuck advised. "We're on a tagging operation. For research. Best if you head out of the area." He lifted his chin to Tyson and Denny. "We've gotta get moving."

"Oh, sure. Yeah." Wade planted his hands on his

hips and studied the horizon. I'm on the hunt for the perfect picture today."

"Good luck with that," Tyson said. "Be safe."

Chuck started the truck and they were moving out.

"You too," Wade called after them, making note of the license plate as the truck lumbered away, the ATV following close behind.

When they were out of sight, Wade radioed back to headquarters and waited for a reply. His temper was barely in check and he needed a minute before confronting Leah. Unfortunately, the only response was static.

He checked his cell phone next and couldn't get a signal.

The cabin door opened and Leah stepped out. "Nothing helpful inside."

"You should've stayed put." His jaw was cramping as he ground his teeth. "You could've been caught."

"I wasn't. Thanks for distracting them."

He couldn't have this argument right now.

"We have a new reference point to add to the file," she said.

"Yay," he said with a distinct lack of enthusiasm. "I've got the license plate," he told her. "And first names."

He tried the radio again as they searched the clearing and he took several pictures of the impressions left by the truck tires. There was no guarantee any sort of crime scene unit could get out here but he didn't want to wreck the scene if he could help it.

She was searching around where the truck had been parked. "And a cell phone!" she called.

"Has to be the guy taking selfies."

"It's locked," she grumbled. "Maybe someone else can unlock it for us." She held it out to him.

"Surely someone on your team or mine can do something with it. Maybe we can make some progress if we can get it open for an emergency call."

She blew out a gusty sigh. "Good point."

He reached out and rested his hands on her shoulders and held her steady. "I know you're mad that we didn't just grab the wolves. But we'll catch up with them at the campground."

"I hope you're right. This obviously isn't their first time around. But it is their first time going against us directly," Leah said. "The tarps they used to get the wolves away from the attack site are in a pile inside. And a box of tranquilizer darts too. I took pictures."

"Good. We'd better get after them. I'll get the ATV."

"And then what?" she asked. "They're getting away with the wolves and we didn't get the GPS tracking tag on the truck."

"We'll know soon enough if they're headed for the campground. Right now, we follow and log their progress. It's not like they'll make much better time off-road in these conditions than we can."

"True," she agreed reluctantly. Pulling her scarf up around her face, she started following the truck on foot.

When he caught up with her after retrieving the ATV, she seemed lost in her own thoughts, but she climbed onto the vehicle and they kept going.

He was concerned once more that she was crying but the last time he'd worried she had been laughing. So he chose to believe that the sniffles he heard were about the cold windy weather rather than emotions.

Everything about her screamed tough. Her every action was decisive and in control. He was not going to handle this well if she turned emotional on him now.

He tested Tyson's phone when they crested the next rise, checking for a signal, to no avail. "Shove this into the pack," he said, preparing to press forward. "It's a brick right now."

She did as he asked while he checked the radio. This time they got an answer from headquarters and it was Justice on watch. Wade gave their current location and relayed all the information about the men they'd seen with the wolves, including the make, model, and license plate on the truck.

"We'll get everyone on this," Justice promised. "Here and in Chicago."

Clearly his brother had learned about Leah's true employer and the impromptu partnership.

"Can they send up a drone?" Leah rubbed her arms. "That would give us a big advantage."

Wade relayed the question and they waited almost a full minute before Justice replied. "Consensus is you're too far out of range. You'll have to keep pursuing on foot. Do you have enough supplies?"

"Supplies are good," Wade confirmed. "Thanks for the GPS tags. We'll look for another opportunity to tag the truck."

"You're welcome," Justice said. "I don't like leaving you out there alone."

"We're not alone. We have each other," Wade said, his gaze tangling with Leah's.

She cocked her head, clearly not sure what to make of that. Then she turned away, as if she could see over the terrain straight to the truck carrying the wolves.

"Get in touch if you learn anything," Wade said.

"Count on it," Justice replied. "I know you're doing fine, but I can airlift you out," Justice said. "You've gone above and beyond, here. This intel is plenty to work with. Let me come get you."

The urgency in Justice's voice was unusual. It caught Leah's attention as well. Her gaze locked with his and she studied him intently.

"Up to you," he said to Leah. "We could head back and let the authorities take it from here. These guys won't make it out of the park with everyone on the lookout."

"I wish you were right." She shook her head. "They can. They've done it before. We have to try and make the campground at least. It's the only lead and the best chance of tailing them to the breeder. I'm not going back without those wolves."

With a nod, Wade toggled the radio button and turned down Justice's offer. "That's a negative, Justice. We are good and we are proceeding. Once we have control of the situation you can definitely airlift us out."

"Be safe," Justice said and signed off.

Wade dropped the radio into his pocket when Leah jumped on top of him. Her momentum carried them over the ATV as bullets churned up the snow all around them.

Seconds later, silence reigned and it seemed the assault was over.

The vehicle had toppled to its side. Steam rose from the motor and the tires in the air spun lazily. She wondered if it was still operational.

He'd check. Soon. In a minute. Right now, with

Leah's body sprawling over him from shoulder to thigh, the situation was just about perfect.

It didn't seem to matter that they were bundled up in cold weather gear or that some murderous idiot had just opened fire on them. This close to her, her scent surrounding him, his body responded in predictable ways.

She levered up on her hands, her eyes roaming over his face. Her hair had come loose, the dark silk spilling over her shoulder. "You're scowling."

No surprise there. Because he was pissed as hell. Furious. "That was a critical error," he said through gritted teeth.

Confused, she asked, "Which part? Me saving your ass or—"

"Them." He cut her off. "Them shooting at you," he clarified. "That won't go unpunished." The attack was attempted murder and Wade intended to make the entire gang pay.

"They were shooting at us." Her brow furrowed. "What are you thinking?"

He could hardly share the full nature of his thoughts, so he shared those that aligned with her focus. "I'm thinking I'm all in. Together we will put that damned gang out of business."

Her frown eased and her lips curled into a smile. "I could kiss you for saying that."

"I could kiss you for saving my life," he said.

"That makes us quite the mutual admiration

society." She started to back up, bracing her hands on his shoulders.

He caught her, gently rolling her under him. "About that kiss. I was serious." Slowly he brought his mouth a breath away from hers. Waited for her to come to her senses and shove him back on his ass.

She wound her hands around his neck and pulled him closer. Shifted so he rested in the cradle of her thighs. Her lips were cold and hot all at once. It was the most ridiculous sensation and the best damn kiss of his life. He didn't want it to end and he took her soft, throaty moan as an invitation to continue.

He swept his tongue past her lips, tasted her. And was pretty sure if the bullet had found him, he'd landed in heaven.

CHAPTER 6

SHE WAS KISSING WADE, a man she'd just met. She didn't know anything about him, other than he worked with Stone's new protection division. Yet his lips felt completely familiar. His taste and heat were the answers to a longing that burned deep inside. The weight of his body covering hers felt absolutely right. Her hands, despite the gloves, seemed to know him.

For a lovely, glorious moment, nothing else existed.

Until she remembered they were lying in fresh snow and she was out here for a purpose. Someone had been shooting at them just a few minutes ago. She opened her eyes and the sunlight set the snow sparkling. It was a pretty backdrop for the overturned ATV.

"They're gone." She hoped so at any rate. The

shooting had stopped and it was quiet again. Her eyes locked with his mouth and she started to kiss him again. "Oh, no. I'm sorry," she sputtered, scooting out from under him.

The sudden lack of his body heat made everything feel colder, the chill sliding down into her bones.

"Sorry for saving my life or…" He left it to her to fill in the blank.

She glared at him. "Sorry for the kiss. That was totally inappropriate."

He sat there in the snow, looking up at her as if just now seeing her for the first time. Relaxed, he was more handsome than ever. She mentally leaped back from that train of thought.

"You regret it?" he asked.

Not one bit. "Yes." Biggest fib of her life. "Yes, of course I do. I promise it won't happen again."

He stood up in one fluid motion and dusted the snow from his pants. "My loss."

She didn't believe him. It was just a kiss. Hot and exciting—and she was not supposed to be thinking about it. "We're here to do a job." She stood as well. "I guess everything sort of snuck up on me."

"Like surviving yet another attack?"

"Exactly. I dragged you into this. It's bad enough without more, um, personal complications. I mean—"

"Stop, Leah. It's fine." His tone, grim and annoyed, finally cut through her churning thoughts. "I don't need your apologies." He took a step closer and bent his head until his nose nearly brushed hers. "I enjoyed kissing you."

His breath was warm on her cheek. The slightest shift would bring her mouth to his once more. "You did?" She gazed into his eyes and the sincerity was almost as shocking as being shot at again. "Um."

She backed up, moving around the ATV, looking for damage. Looking for anything to break his spell. "I think we got lucky."

"I know we did," Wade said as he righted the vehicle and checked it out. "All the tires are intact, only a few surface scratches.

An icy awareness trickled down her spine. The vehicle was spared because the man behind the rifle had been aiming for her and Wade. It was a sobering thought. She didn't want Wade to be hurt because his boss ordered him to partner up with her.

"Most of the bullets went over our heads or sprayed wide to the front," he observed.

"Well hooray for bad aim."

Wade snorted.

"They must have tracked Tyson's phone to us," she said.

He grunted. "Could just as easily have waited to see if we followed them," he countered.

"Did you mean it about not going back?"

He shot her an incredulous look. "Did you hear me order an airlift?"

"No. No, I just didn't mean to drag anyone else into my mess," she said. "I know what our bosses told us last night, but this couldn't be what you expected."

"First off, this isn't your mess. Those men are to blame, not you."

"Right. Of course." She was rattled, more than a little. "I knew what I was getting into." Why couldn't she stop talking? "It just that, well, if you want Justice to pick you up, that's fine. I'm safe and I can take it from here."

He folded his arms over his chest and stared her down. "You think I'm leaving you out here against a crew willing to kill to get away with their prize? Who the hell do you take me for?"

"Um. That's just it. I don't know you. We were thrown together and..." She lost her train of thought as something shifted in his gaze. Heat or humor, she couldn't sort it out.

"You know my lips well enough."

He was teasing. Had to be. And she was being remarkably slow on the uptake. "About that." She cleared her throat and somehow managed not to touch her mouth again. "I'm sor—"

"Do not apologize to me again," he warned. Any flicker of joking was gone. "Let's see what we can salvage."

"You're really sticking?"

He positively glowered at her. "I came to Yellowstone with my team to do a job. We search, we rescue, and we recover when necessary. We do not give up and we do not let bad guys escape. Whether or not you want me involved, I'm all in until it's over."

"Thanks." She couldn't think of anything more profound or helpful.

Without a word, they quickly sorted through the gear, looking for anything damaged. It was a tremendous relief to find the tent had been spared, though the emergency blankets had a few holes. Most of the water and food had survived the attack and the rifle and handgun were fine.

"I want to get away from here," he said. "Make it look like we left the disabled ATV and are running scared."

"Fine by me." She slung the rifle over her shoulder, while Wade took the handgun. "Hiking to the campground is a big ask." She hated to admit to any kind of limit, but he had a right to know she could be a liability.

"We're not doing that, I promise." They cherry-picked a few essentials and set off in the opposite direction of the gang and the campground marked on the GPS they'd taken from Ronnie.

"Why wouldn't they come back and make sure they killed us?"

"We're small fish," Wade replied. "As you've said, escaping with their cargo is the real goal. They think we're stranded at the very least. And that assumption can work in our favor."

She started to protest, then snapped her mouth closed when his words sunk in.

"Good."

They left the ATV behind and hiked to the west, as if heading for the main road that wound through this area of the park. It was subtle but she could feel Wade guiding them in a big loop, over terrain that would hide their actual intended path.

"You think hiking in a circle will fool them?" she asked.

"Yes. They aren't watching us. Not since we went over the ATV anyway."

Her neck prickled and there was a twitch between her shoulder blades as she waited for a bullet to slam into her from any direction. It didn't feel right pretending the gang wasn't a threat. As the minutes turned to an hour, it was clear Wade was right. Getting away with the wolves was more important than a couple of people out tooling around in the snow.

She felt heat creeping up into her face thinking

about those men watching her make out with Wade. It wasn't as if they'd put on a show. The gang had cleared out quickly. Even with binoculars or a rifle sight, what had happened was between her and Wade.

"Don't get me wrong, I'm all for wolf conservation," Wade said. "I understand your passion for animals and wildlife, but why are you so bent on taking out this particular crew?"

She trudged along, her feet feeling heavy after the ups and downs of various adrenaline rushes. She wasn't pretending to feel defeated, she actually was worried about failure. The wolves had been right there, almost within reach of rescue.

Almost. That was the key. They were heading for the closed campground, which was a much better place to try and recover those wolves. Maybe she could take the truck and leave the gang stranded. Assuming Wade would be able and willing to guard them until authorities arrived. She discarded the idea. Not a great plan, pitting one man against three, especially with no certainty about when backup would get there.

"I'm glad you're here," she said suddenly. "And this particular gang is a thorn in my side. I've been trying to make inroads into their operation for over a year. Poaching is a general problem," she continued. "Taking out one crew doesn't solve the entire issue."

"Puts a damn dent in it and makes someone else think twice," Wade interjected.

"Exactly my hope," she agreed. "My mom first caught wind of the problem of wolves and hybrids being passed off as a new breed. I shared her concerns with my bosses, and asked them to put their researchers on it. We've been trying to investigate. Just over a year ago, I was working at a rodeo and heard more rumors about wolf dogs. That got me transitioned to Yellowstone. Failure on this case is not an option for me."

"You must be even more motivated now."

"After the carnage at the capture site, you're damned right." She paused for some water. "The wolf packs of Yellowstone are natural predators and opportunists. They're also beautiful, powerful animals." And yes, it definitely hurt her heart to see them locked up in cages in the back of that truck.

"Did your mom see the hybrids herself?"

"She did. Two hybrids came into her practice. People who didn't know better about the kind of dog they had adopted. They were able to pinpoint the breeder who'd sold the animals and shut him down. He claimed he'd purchased wolves that had been captured by ranchers—unnamed of course—further west.

"So that was a dead end."

She shook her head. "Would've been, except veterinarians have a professional network that can move quick as lightning when word gets out of something like this. There are some really ugly people with some really bad exotic pet habits."

"Can I ask who you were protecting at the rodeo?"

"Follow the circuit?"

"A little." He shrugged.

She chuckled. "I could tell you, but then I have to kill you."

He reared back in mock horror. "Isn't that supposed to be my line?"

"Are you admitting you were a spy during your military career?"

"In a manner of speaking. The 10th Mountain Division has a long and storied history of unique operations and rescues. We even work with veterinarians sometimes."

"Well lucky you," she said. "The Guardian Agency is all about discretion and need-to-know status."

"What about the client? You must've left some poor bull rider harassed by buckle bunnies to fend for himself."

"Well, that's a fine fishing expedition you've got there, Mr. Fielding." She laughed. "But my agency also takes security seriously. They did not leave the client hanging when they transferred me."

"I'm so relieved to hear it."

"Me too, actually. I liked my client and enjoyed the protection detail."

"Are you a rodeo fan?" he asked.

"I guess so. I consider myself more of an animal lover. There are times when I root for the bull or horse rather than the cowboy taking the ride."

"You've got a mean streak," he observed.

"No, I have a justice streak a mile wide," she corrected. "Same as you," she added after a minute.

"You sound pretty sure of yourself when it comes to me."

Did he really think it wasn't obvious? "Well, there are a few factors," she said. "Starting with you being part of the local Brotherhood Protectors team. Stone wouldn't have you if you didn't share his values or lacked integrity."

"Can't argue with that," Wade said. "But you can't heap all military service people into one box. We aren't clones."

"Of course not. Some of you smile," she teased.

With his face mask pulled aside, she could see his expression was almost amused. Maybe that was outright amused by his standards.

Her legs were burning from the effort of the rugged terrain by the time he aimed them back toward the ATV.

"Do you think it's possible to get a lifetime worth of steps in one day?" she wondered.

"Not sure it works that way," he replied.

"Besides, I can't see you just sitting down for the rest of your life."

"After this, I might be persuaded to sit down for a good long time," she confessed.

He stopped, his gaze raking over her. "Do you need to rest?"

"No," she replied with renewed determination. "Forgive my griping. We need to rescue those wolves and break up this operation."

"Hardly griping," he said. "This isn't easy for me either. Plus, you started at a deficit spending the other night under a root ball."

He made a good point, but she didn't want to wallow in it. And thanks to his timely arrival, she'd spent last night in a warm bed after a good, restorative meal. "Regardless, complaining won't speed this along."

They walked for several more minutes in a comfortable quiet, both of them alert to any threat while they appreciated the stunning, wild scenery.

"Do your parents know what you're actually doing for the Guardian Agency?"

"Not exactly. They know I shifted career interests after dropping out of vet school and work for a Chicago law firm now. I'm not exactly a disappointment to them, but every once in a while they forget to hide how much they wish I was preparing to take over mom's practice."

"Why did you drop out of vet school?"

She sighed. It was her own fault for mentioning it. "Suffice it to say I was accused of mishandling drugs during an internship."

"Who the hell tried to pin that on you?"

She stumbled, caught her balance and gaped at him. "Why do you assume I didn't do it?"

He scowled. "Because I've spent more than ten minutes with you."

He said it as if that explained everything. But it didn't. People who knew her better than he did right now weren't as confident that she was on the right side of the line.

He scoffed. "Come on. Your integrity shines like the sun, Leah. No way you mishandled controlled substances."

"Thanks." It was as if Wade had magically lifted that burden right off her shoulders. The baggage of doubts and skepticism she hadn't been able to let go of was just…gone. "I mean it. Your confidence is more than I got at the time." Only her parents had stood by her. "It was a junior vet in the practice who saw me as an excellent scapegoat. By the time I cleared my name the window on vet school had closed. I had to find new opportunities."

Wade stopped, pulled off his sunglasses and studied her. "I'm sorry, Leah. That had to really suck."

She nodded, more than a little overwhelmed by his sincerity. "Thanks. It was a hard year." Then she started moving again, because if she didn't, she might launch herself into his arms and that would be about the most needy and unprofessional thing she'd ever done.

"It took you a year to clear your name?" He scrambled up a tumble of rocks, reaching back to help her over the slippery rise. "When we finish here, do you want me to track him down and beat him up for you?"

"If only." She laughed. As far as she could recall it was the first time she'd laughed over that ordeal. "It's water under the bridge. Besides, I like my job." On solid ground, she stomped to ease the achiness in her feet.

"Well, whatever we find at the closed campground, we'll have good shelter thanks to the supply drop. I can't guarantee a five-star meal but it'll be high-calorie."

"Definitely need calories after all of this," she agreed. She grabbed his arm as he started forward. "Wait! Do you hear that?"

He listened, but shook his head. She held up a hand, so he'd stay quiet. Then the sound reached them again. A pitiful wailing carried on the breeze, underscored by the faint sounds of a revving engine.

"That has to be them," she said.

"No way," Wade disagreed. "They should be well away from here now."

"Maybe they backtracked to make sure we were gone."

He was frowning as he crouched down, staying low as he inched toward the top of the rise to get a view of the valley. She crept right along with him.

"It's them," she grumbled. "If they don't do something soon, every predator in the area will descend on that truck tonight."

"Looks like they got caught in something under the snow," Wade observed, his tone neutral.

Two of the three men were attempting to get the right rear wheel free of some sort of hazard hidden by the snow. The driver had his door open and was yelling instructions. On the far side of the truck, a herd of bison kept an eye on the situation.

The wolves were restless, the weight of their cages compounding the trouble.

The gang was right there, begging to be arrested. "Can we take them?"

"I don't think so," Wade replied. "We know they're well-armed and there's no way to get from here to there with any element of surprise."

He was right, though she didn't want to admit it. "If I covered you with the rifle—"

"No, Leah." He turned, his expression earnest. "Our best bet is the campground. Out here, they'll see us coming. They could scatter, kill the wolves, or get free and drive off before we can move into range."

She knew he was right, but she didn't have to like it. "It's moments like this when the size of this park is a disadvantage," she murmured. "Impossible to dial 911 and expect a response. And yet without this big park so many animals would be gone."

"In this case we are the emergency responders."

"You just said we can't charge in and take prisoners."

His mouth twitched into a half-smile. "No, we can't do that. We can call in the current location." He reached for his radio to do just that.

She watched, fuming as the effort to free the truck was paused to deal with the crying wolves. The driver hauled a cooler out of the cab. Each wolf was given a hunk of what must have been raw meat loaded with a sedative, since the animals stopped crying within minutes.

Someone with significant experience had equipped and instructed the thieves. Anger simmered, threatening to erupt into a wildfire of rage. Her hand curled around the rifle she carried.

"Easy," Wade said.

"Remind me why we can't just disable them and force them to sit in the snow until the authorities arrive?"

"I like your bloodthirsty tendencies. But shooting from here is a waste of good bullets. It could set off the bison herd. Moreover, going on the offensive now would undermine your goal of taking down the illegal breeding operation."

"We can make them talk, right? They should want to turn over the person calling the shots. None of them look like they would fare well in prison."

Wade rolled to his back, smothering a laugh in the crook of his arm. "You make a good point," he gasped. "I promise we're not letting them get away. When it's time to shoot, I'll let you."

"Fine." She released the gun, willing to listen. "If you've got a plan in mind, now is the time to share."

CHAPTER 7

HE DIDN'T HAVE a real plan, that was the problem. But Wade knew that going in hot right now would be more than the two of them could handle. There was no solution that didn't turn into a shootout, putting the wolves and Leah in harm's way.

Not to mention what the bison might do.

He hadn't been in Yellowstone long but it was a rugged and wild place, and people did not have the right of way. Bison looked slow and sleepy. Sometimes they even appeared cuddly, but Wade knew they were unpredictable and frequently as grumpy as he was.

"Wade, please. We have to do something more."

"I sent in the coordinates. Someone on your team or mine might be able to get more information on the truck and whoever owns it. Maybe that will help us narrow down their destination."

She sighed, clearly frustrated.

He kept watch on the crew wrestling with the truck. Spared a glance for the bison herd. And continued to scan the horizon for any sign of the natural predators that might be interested in the distressed wolves.

A big bull bison finally gave the truck his full attention, taking several strides toward the vehicle and the men working to get the tire free. The men weren't giving him the same respect, too consumed by their predicament. "Trust me, we don't want to get involved now. Not with that bison checking them out."

Her eyes gleamed, ready for battle. "My money is on the bison."

"Only a sucker would take that bet."

She chuckled. "Fine. We wait for the campground. It fits their current heading and it offers good shelter."

"Also out of the way if the wolves get noisy again."

"True."

She didn't elaborate and he glanced over, trying not to smile. When Leah was deep in thought, her whole body went still. He found it endearing. And a little scary. What required her entire body to focus? "What is it?" he prompted.

"The breeder has to be close," she said.

"You mean in the park?"

"Yes. I think so. At the very least close to the borders. The capture gang can't keep the wolves drugged indefinitely. Too many risks. Those animals are worth a fortune."

He couldn't argue. "Fastest way out is to fly, and any plan to rendezvous with a helo would require a big aircraft. And I wouldn't want to move those cages." He scrubbed at his face. Even if she was right, searching Yellowstone was a monumental task.

"Do you think we can get ahead of them?" she asked.

"Doubtful." He pointed. The men had the truck rolling again.

"I'm sure they're taking the most direct route possible. We'll have to be careful as we follow."

"They're too arrogant to keep an eye out for us." Her lip curled into a sneer. "I'm not giving up."

"We aren't giving up," he corrected. "And their arrogance gives us a narrow advantage. Let's keep going. We'll keep the others informed of our progress. Between Justice and Chelsea, they'll let us know when they can ride in and support our rescue efforts." He watched her eyes narrow. "What are you thinking?"

"I'm wishing we could string them up at the gate like they did with pirates back in the day." She stopped, her eyes going wide. "Whoa. Sorry. I really am bloodthirsty."

He laughed, free to let loose now that they were alone. Rolling to his feet, he held out a hand to her. "A beautiful woman who knows how to shoot, with a fierce streak to go right along with her sense of justice and love of wildlife." He whistled. "You might just be the perfect woman, Leah Williams."

"Not even close," she said, laughing with him. "Working undercover is basically lying to friends, family, and strangers alike. Hardly the picture of perfection."

They hiked straight toward the ATV and he pushed the pace, knowing she was getting desperate to make something happen. "You aren't lying to hurt anyone or to advance your own agenda," he pointed out. "I know what it's like when doing the right thing requires some questionable tactics."

At the ATV, she paused at his side rather than climb back into the seat behind him. "Do you like who you are?"

"Yes." It surprised him to be so certain. "There was a time when I struggled. Right after my dad died."

"I'm sorry for your loss." Her gaze filled with compassion. Not pity, but something far more acceptable.

"It's been almost twenty years," he said. "But thank you. We all felt it. He was our foundation. Wasn't sure my mom was going to recover. It rocked Justice too. My dad was the closest thing he had to a real father."

She lifted a hand, as if she wanted to touch him, but didn't follow through. "Can I ask what happened to your dad?"

"We were on a ski trip. The big winter vacation. My sister and mom were waiting at the lodge while Dad and I were taking on a more challenging route." Feeling his heart race, he paused to pull himself together. "We got caught in an avalanche."

"Oh my God, Wade. That's awful."

He took her hand and squeezed. "We were rescued right away. But he died from his injuries a couple days later at the hospital."

She hugged him. Not pity, pure support. And the rest of the story poured out of him. "I thought Mom would be furious. That she'd blame me. I had insisted on one more run on a tough slope. But you know what? Even in her grief, she never did. Going home, dealing with his absence day after day..." He shook his head. "Telling Justice was the hardest thing I ever had to do."

"I can't imagine."

She rubbed his shoulders, back and forth, soothing him in a way he'd never allowed anyone else. Why was he baring his soul to her? He needed to drop the topic and get her focused again on the wolves. Instead, he told her more.

"After that, Justice practically moved in and

became more of a brother than ever. Sometimes I think he's closer to Mom than I am." Wade sighed. "He never admitted it, but I've always believed Dad's death pushed Justice into the military."

"What do you mean?"

"The Army offered him a clean break after high school graduation. He didn't have money for college or the grades for a decent scholarship."

"It's a smart solution," she sympathized.

"Yeah, well, I couldn't let him go into the Army alone, so we went to the recruiting office together. And when I got excited about a search and rescue career path, he wouldn't let me do that alone."

"And the rest is history," she beamed. "Lucky for me."

Her big smile was prettier than a summer sunrise and more heartwarming than the first autumn fire in the hearth.

"From what I've heard since your team came to Yellowstone, you have a solid success record." Her gaze drifted out over the valley they needed to cross.

"We do our best." He paused, making sure he had her full attention. "This will be a success too, Leah. You and I are going to get home in one piece, along with those wolves."

"You really believe that," she said, incredulous.

"That's right."

"Even without a plan?"

Caught, he tried to laugh it off. "Right now, the best plan is to trail them, report in, and when it's time, we help take down the gang."

"All right." She studied the valley once more. "We're running out of time and daylight."

"So let's get moving," he said. "Sticking with them means we'll likely spend the night in the elements in order to be close enough to put a tracker on the truck and stay on their trail. Can you handle another night out here?"

Her eyes flashed and he held up his hands in surrender before she could answer. "Forget I asked. Clearly, you can handle anything."

"Pretty much," she said with a great deal of conviction. "And I thought your brother gave us plenty of survival gear."

"He did," Wade confirmed. "It won't be comfortable, but it can be done."

"Comfort's overrated," she declared.

Her bravado was amusing as well as contagious. "All right," he caved to her idea. "Let's go make sure the thieves are only taking shelter and not making a handoff in that campground."

And on the ride, he'd enjoy every minute of having her body pressed close to him. High points were few and far between in conditions like this and after that zinger of a kiss, he felt like he'd earned the right to savor every moment.

IT WAS full dark by the time they reached the campground. Knowing the destination and hoping to avoid another run-in with the truck, they'd taken a circuitous route and had to leave the ATV well behind to prevent getting caught. Leah had spent the afternoon trying not to envision the worst-case scenario: that the gang would change plans and stop elsewhere for the night.

But there they were, exactly at the point Ronnie had saved on his GPS. Leah clenched her jaw to prevent her teeth from chattering as she gazed at the truck in the central campground. The gang had tossed a tarp over the truck bed, likely to prevent their cargo from being seen on any closed-circuit security system that might be active within the campground.

In the meantime, the three men were taking advantage, opening a cabin and making themselves at home. Leah rubbed her hands together and then tucked them between her knees, trying not to envy the men and their sturdy shelter from the elements.

Her bloodthirsty tendencies were surging to the fore. A few minutes ago, she'd even suggested burning down their cabin. It was a bad idea for a number of reasons and yet just imagining the heat that kind of fire would generate was somehow comforting.

Maybe Wade was right and the cold had compromised her critical thinking.

"Do we have to camp outside?" she asked. "What if we take a cabin on the other side of the campground?"

"No." He squashed her hope of a hot shower and a decent bed after a day bumping around on the ATV. "We'd be sitting ducks if we tried that."

She knew he was right. But when this was over, she was going to find a fancy spa and pamper herself for a week.

"You are absolutely sure we can't just let those wolves go?"

"Positive," she replied. "Not just because Chelsea would kill me. We're too far from their pack. They could get into all kinds of trouble on their way back to their known rendezvous point." She tucked her chin deeper into the warmth of her scarf. "I understand why you want to. It's killing me to see them in those cages."

"Okay I get it," he said. "And if the wolves are gone, it's unlikely those guys will lead us to the breeding site."

Also a factor she'd been considering.

"We won't screw this up after coming this far."

She was grateful the scarf hid the shock on her face. "Thank you."

"For what?" He scowled.

The furrow between his eyebrows made her

want to smile. "For trusting me." Sometimes it felt like the ghosts of those accusations in vet school would never release her.

Wade gripped her shoulders. "Leah, I'm not a punk with my own agenda. I'm your partner in this. You can count on me."

"Right. I know and I'm grateful."

That frown only deepened. "Check the radio," he said gruffly.

She did. "We have a good signal."

"Let's not waste it," he urged. "Notify the research center first."

She hadn't thought her heart could melt in the freezing conditions, but his putting the wolves first did it. There was a soft puddle of goo in her ribcage as she made the call.

Naturally, Chelsea was at the research center waiting for an update. Leah explained, "The wolves are subdued and groggy. We haven't heard any whining or vocalizing in the past hour. We saw the gang drug them a few hours ago when they were crying. We'll keep monitoring," she finished.

With a heartfelt thanks, Chelsea urged them to be safe and signed off.

Leah clutched the radio in her hands. "What now?"

Wade's eyes smiled. "I'll update Stone and then we set up camp for the night."

While he radioed his boss, she looked around

for a good spot, choosing a place well away from the cabin and downwind of the wolves. They found a secluded area with a thick screen of trees on a rise above the central campground. From what she could see, it should make for a relatively easy trek down the hill to tag the truck and they'd know if the gang moved out in the night.

Wade pulled a hand warmer out of his pack. "Sorry we can't have a fire."

"Are you kidding? If we did that we might as well issue an invitation for them to come up here and harass us. Or worse."

"True. Enough of a risk pitching the tent," he added.

But it was too cold to survive without it. Working together they soon had the tent up and ready despite the darkness. It would be a tight squeeze for two of them, but the shared body heat and emergency blankets were keys to surviving the night.

Nearby owls called from the trees, staking territory while prey scurried through the snowy underbrush. All things considered, it wasn't a bad campsite. Before ducking into the tent for a break from the weather, they camouflaged their location with more branches and forest debris.

Her hands were starting to feel normal again and she was halfway through a protein bar when the shouting started down near the cabin where the gang was holed up. She and Wade slipped out of the tent and crouched in a place where they could watch and listen without being seen.

The cabin door was wide open and one of the men appeared. Staggering backward, his arms windmilling through the square of light from the cabin, he landed hard on his butt.

The driver stepped out of the cabin, a gun in his hand.

"He has a gun," Leah whispered.

"I see it." Beside her Wade's body might as well have been carved from granite.

"Take it easy, Chuck." Tyson rolled to his feet and dusted the snow off his jeans. "It's not like I knew the guy. Who would? He just walked up outta nowhere."

"And you didn't think that was weird? He and the woman were following us."

"Come on." Tyson laughed. "You don't know that."

Chuck spewed a long litany of Tyson's failings. "You're useless. Losing your phone. Getting caught on a camera."

"What? No way."

"You. Got caught. On your last delivery." Chuck stalked Tyson, lifting the gun. "Boss got wind of someone trying to identify who delivered a hybrid in Indiana. You know better."

"Cameras are everywhere--"

"Not here," Chuck cut him off. "You're done."

Tyson raised his hands. "Chill, man. You need—"

"This isn't about me," Chuck said, his tone lethal. "Where's your phone, Tyson?"

"Who the hell knows? A bison probably crushed it by now," he complained. "Gimme a break. We're almost done."

Leah knew what was coming. As she watched Chuck, she knew he was about to kill Tyson. "Where's the other guy?" she wondered. "Denny?"

There was movement in the truck bed and a ripple of unease shivered near the tent. The wolves, along with the nocturnal animals in the area, sensed the trouble. Survival instincts urged the wildlife to seek shelter, but the wolves were stuck.

Frustrated, her own instincts had her leaning forward, ready to intervene. Wade stopped her, one firm hand on her shoulder.

She glanced away from the scene below and he shook his head. "We can't let him shoot."

Suddenly, Wade grabbed her, pulling her down with him to the ground. "Don't look."

But she couldn't look away. Tyson's body jerked as the first bullet hit his chest. He stumbled back, hands coming to his belly, before he was struck twice more. He dropped like a felled tree.

Everything inside her went cold and all of the earlier sounds were simply gone. Just a flat, eerie silence. Though Wade tried to block her view, she stared helplessly as blood flowed from the lifeless body, staining the pale snow.

Suddenly, her ears were ringing so loudly she covered her ears, ducking her face into Wade's chest. "Easy, Leah. Just breathe."

It took some effort, but she managed to do as he asked. Lowering her hands, she clung to him. Wade's hands covered hers. "I'm going down. You stay here."

"But—"

"Please, Leah. We have to get a tracking tag on the truck."

He was right. That was their best hope of finding the person behind this operation. "All right," she murmured.

A moment later, Wade was gone, soundlessly blending with the wilderness. And then another argument erupted in front of the cabin.

"You've lost it man." Denny turned back toward the cabin.

"Hold it! Get back here." Chuck held the gun loosely at his side, showing no signs of remorse. "Get the body out of here."

"Me?" Denny choked. "I'm not burying your mess."

"Do it." Chuck advanced.

"And put i-it where? The ground is frozen solid," Denny argued.

"Cover him with snow or something." Chuck swore. "Who cares? The animals will find him."

Leah pressed her hands to her mouth. She couldn't believe what she was seeing. Worse, she couldn't believe Wade was down there in the thick of it. One wrong move and he might be Chuck's next victim.

And where would that leave her? He'd told her to wait, but she had to do something. Something more than watch Chuck eliminate his gang. Gingerly, she removed the cell phone from her pocket, turned off the flash, and started taking pictures.

The man loomed over Denny, tapping the gun against his thigh. "Do you not appreciate that I just gave you a pay raise? Fifty percent beats the hell out of the twenty-five you started with. Earn your money and get rid of the body."

"Fine. Fine!" Denny shouted. "As soon as you go back inside."

"What? You don't give the orders here."

Denny stood his ground. "You just pumped three bullets into Tyson. I'm not dumb enough to let you do the same to me."

Shock had Leah rattling like a dried leaf. Yes, she'd talked a big game, been blood-thirsty over what this crew had done to the wolf pack, but that was merely emotion. Anger and frustration. Sadness over a senseless loss. She'd never truly intended to harm the crew, just get them into custody.

Where was Wade?

Under the watchful gazes of the caged wolves, Denny dragged Tyson's body away, into the shadows between two cabins. She couldn't see him, but she could hear him muttering and moving around.

Where was Wade?

Denny slowly trudged back to the cabin, his head down. The woods seemed to go quiet and she waited for any sign of Wade.

At last, she saw movement. Slow and silent until he stepped into full view. It was all she could do to hold still.

"You okay?" he asked, stretching out on his belly beside her.

"Not really." She rolled to her back. "I took pictures."

"Good." He didn't speak for some time. "I tagged the truck."

"Good."

"Come on. Let's get into the tent before we freeze."

Within the protection of the tent, he looked at the pictures. "Not bad. I'm not sure it's enough, but it is a start," he said. "We'll send this with our update as soon as they move out."

All she could do was nod in agreement. A

tremor slammed through her body and she hugged her knees to her chest, desperate to regain some control. "I don't want to die out here." Shameful as it was, her courage had fled with that first gunshot. "I'm scared," she confessed.

"I'd be worried if you weren't," Wade soothed, his voice a low whisper. "Hang in and stick with me. We'll get through this."

She appreciated his kindness and compassion in the face of her weakness. "I just need…I need…" But she didn't know what she needed. She was out of her league.

"Hydrate," he suggested, pressing a water bottle into her hands.

She drank, but it didn't fix anything. Nothing could. A man was dead. Yes, he'd been engaged in criminal behavior, but still. He'd been alive and vibrant one second and dead the next. No chance to redeem himself.

A pack of crackers appeared in front of her. "To settle your stomach," Wade said.

"Thanks." She really should be taking care of herself, but standing by as a silent witness to murder seemed to have vaporized her independence.

Eventually, Leah realized she was cuddled up with Wade, her back pressed to his chest and his legs stretched along hers. Her body quivered, despite the steady, gentle strokes of his hands over her arms. "We can't let him get away with this," she said, her voice trembling.

"He'll pay." Wade's chest lifted on a deep breath. "I promise you, Leah, justice will be served. They'll all pay for their crimes against you, against the wolves, and for Tyson's murder, too." The menacing undercurrent of his vow was unmistakable. A tone that probably left people shaking only comforted her. She didn't have the energy to unpack why that was, but she wrapped the awareness around her heart like a warm blanket. "Thank you."

His lips brushed her temple.

"You should sleep," she said at last, moving out of his embrace. "I can keep watch."

"You sure? You haven't gotten much real sleep."

She nodded. "I've got this." In the dim light, it was hard to see his eyes, but she heard the concern in his mellow voice. "I'll wake you if there's trouble."

She wouldn't be getting any quality sleep until this was over and she was back home. Not in Chicago, or on the road with a client, but in her apartment in West Yellowstone. It hadn't really felt like home until now. Seemed she was more attached to this area than she'd thought.

"Do that." They changed places in the cramped tent so she was closer to the entrance. As he passed, Wade caught her chin between his fingers and pressed a fast, sweet kiss to her lips. "Whatever is going on in your head, remember that you are strong, you're remarkable, and we will get through this. Together."

Leaving her with tingling lips, he slid under the emergency blanket, pillowing his head on his arm, his back to her.

Despite everything, she felt herself smiling. He might be the search and rescue expert with all of the military experience, but he was human. Helping him by pulling her own weight was the least she could do considering all he had done for her since being tasked with finding her.

She studied the campground through the narrow slit in the tent flap. The truck hadn't moved, the wolves were quiet, and the cabin where Chuck and Denny were hiding was dark. She rested her hands on the guns Wade had tucked up against the tent wall on either side of the flap.

Thinking through their plan to follow the truck to the breeding site, she wished for another way. One without quite as many unknowns. What if the tracker failed and they lost the truck? What if they ran out of fuel for the ATV? Maybe she should sneak down there and disable the truck. Siphon the gas out of the tank or slice a tire. Would that be enough to delay Chuck and Denny long enough to get the sheriff out here?

Not likely. With the access road covered in

snow, the fastest way to reach this campground was by helicopter. The campground facilities probably had fuel stored on site. Possibly even other vehicles. Those two men were determined to turn over those wolves and get their payday. This clearly wasn't their first time and she was sure they had contingency plans for any number of problems.

Like an unexpected murder.

She kept seeing Tyson's body jerk and fall. Even with her eyes open. She couldn't put it out of her mind. Tears threatened, even knowing she needed clear vision to keep watch. Pressing her lips together, she ordered herself not to cry over a man who had stolen wolves.

Behind her, Wade shifted. "Aw, honey. Come here."

She twisted and he lifted the blanket and invited her under, moving so he was between the tent flap and her. He didn't turn his back this time. No, his strong body spooned up close behind her. Stirred her senses and sparked some seriously hot fantasies. The heat she needed, but this wasn't the right time to lose her head over her sexy rescuer.

Their kisses earlier danced through her mind and it took significant willpower to lock down the memory. She had to be suffering from some kind of stress infatuation. "I was keeping watch," she protested, determined to remind herself why they were out here.

"And you did great. Now it's my turn. I'll stay alert while you sleep." He slipped one arm under her head and draped the other over her waist.

The effect was incredibly intimate, despite the layers of cold weather gear between them. She hadn't shared a bed, rustic as this one was, with a man in over a year. Still, there was something deeply comforting about his keeping watch while she slept. His presence alone smoothed the raw edges of her scattered emotions and seemed to bring her back to herself.

Breath by breath, her cold fear for the wolves, her dread that she'd fail to find the illegal breeding site, and the smothering sadness of a life cruelly taken melted away.

CHAPTER 8

WADE WOKE with his arms full of Leah and a rock-hard morning erection. More than the usual morning occurrence. The sweet fragrance of Leah's dark hair scented the air, an effective distraction against what would be a zero-coffee morning. Vying for control of his body, he aimed his thoughts toward everything other than how well she fit with him. Yesterday's kisses hadn't been the smartest move, but he didn't regret a thing. She'd started it anyway, he thought with a smile.

Started something he yearned to finish.

But this wasn't the place and if he'd learned anything about Leah, it was her intense focus on the task. Except when they'd kissed. Then she seemed to forget everything but the two of them. He liked that, the promise of it, probably more than he should.

The faint whimpers of the wolves trapped on the truck carried through the morning and Leah woke with the sound. "Wade?"

"Right here." He couldn't resist curling his body around her for just a second before easing back. "Warm enough?"

"Yes." She carefully rolled to her back. "You're awake," she whispered.

"I am."

"Is it my turn to take the watch?"

"No. It's time to think about how we'll move out without being noticed."

She sat up, her dark eyes full of concern. "It's morning? We agreed to take turns. I can pull my weight."

"I never doubted that," he assured her. "I'm good, I promise." He hadn't done more than doze through the night, but he was rested enough. He didn't think she'd appreciate his explanation that she'd been sleeping so soundly that he couldn't bear to wake her.

She glared at him. He propped himself up on an elbow, bringing his face closer to hers. "How do you feel?"

Her gaze dropped to his mouth and heat spread through him. Those kisses hadn't been a fluke. The attraction was mutual.

"W-we need to be careful," she said.

He wasn't sure if she was talking about the electricity arcing between them or the dangers of the thieves catching them. "We will be." He rummaged around for the cell phone, pulling up the app that tracked the tag he'd put on the truck.

"They're still down there."

She cocked her head. "We can hear them."

"True." He stretched his arms overhead. "But they won't stay here long."

She blinked several times. "Right."

Carefully, to avoid any unwanted attention, they took care of their individual needs and fueled up on the meal bars they'd packed until, at last, Chuck and Denny moved out of the abandoned lodge.

"Still heading east," Leah reported, watching them through the binoculars until the truck and ATV were out of sight.

"We'll need to hang back a little more than you'd like," he warned. "Otherwise they'll spot us out here way too fast."

"Understood."

Breaking camp was quick work when they didn't have to be quiet about it. Hustling back to the ATV, they secured the gear and were soon underway, trailing the truck. Though the truck stayed on the road, the road hadn't been plowed and the going was slow. And there was no way to tell where Denny might wander on his ATV. Wade relied on Leah's reports on the tracking app for any adjustments in their course.

They'd been on the trail for a couple of slow hours when Wade spotted movement up ahead and aimed for the nearest stand of trees. They needed to hide if that was Denny circling back, but shadows and shelter were hard to find in the winter at just past noon on a clear day.

"What is it?" Leah asked, leaning close to his back.

Her body felt good pressed close to his, but it was a distraction he couldn't afford just now. "I think Chuck sent Denny back to find us." Who else would be riding all-out and heading straight for them.

"He's not being subtle about it," she observed. "You think they managed to tag us?"

"I don't see how," Wade replied. "I went over this thing with a fine tooth comb this morning."

They waited as the ATV closed in on their position. The driver was leaning heavily on the front handlebars and the vehicle was swerving as if he couldn't control it.

While he watched, in fascinated horror, the ATV hit a bump in the snow and slid back, the tires coming to a stop when the driver's hand fell from the throttle control. "Stay back," he ordered. Grabbing the first aid kit, he raced out to see how he could help. Some things were just pure instinct and this kind of situation was exactly what Wade was built for.

"It's Denny!" he shouted to Leah. "Injured," he reported as he hauled the man off and away from the ATV.

Leah ran out to join him, skidding to a stop when she saw the bloodstains on his coat. "That's fresh."

Wade looked up. "You okay with blood?"

She dropped to the ground on the other side of Denny. "Of course. Vet school, remember?"

"Vet school?" Denny lurched away from her. "I'm no dog."

"No, you're not," she agreed. "Dogs are worth saving."

Wade snorted. "So is Denny."

"I'll call it in." Leah reached for her radio.

Denny slapped her arm. "No. Don't. He'll hear you."

"Chuck can't monitor all the channels."

"Not him. The boss," Denny wheezed.

"Quiet now," Wade ordered. He shot Leah a warning glare. "Let me get a look at the problem."

Denny dropped back into the snow. "Chuck shot me, that's the problem."

"For what?" Leah queried.

Wade was impressed with the way she seemed to know exactly how to help him open the coat and peel it away from the bleeding wound.

Wounds, plural. "Looks like it went straight through."

"Could I be that lucky?" Denny wondered.

"Let's find out." Wade, with Leah's assistance, rolled Denny onto his side to confirm both entry and exit wounds. "Shot in the back," he said. "Clean through and out the front." Wade opened his kit to clean the wounds.

Leah popped to her feet and checked the ATV.

"How did you piss off Chuck?"

"I got in his face about Tyson. The man was my friend. A goofball at times, but I liked him. He deserved better."

"We all do," Wade agreed. "This is gonna hurt."

Denny sighed.

"Found the bullet," Leah announced, returning from her search of the ATV. "Anything I can wrap it up in?"

"Help yourself to anything that isn't gauze, the stitches kit, or antiseptic solution."

She rooted around, gathered a few items he didn't need, and disappeared again.

"You're gonna just stitch me up and let me go?"

"Something like that," Wade muttered as he worked. Denny hollered at the sting of the cold air and the antiseptic. He argued about stitches, but Wade ignored him.

"Why are you doing this?" Denny mumbled.

"Because he's a good man," Leah replied

emphatically. "Why do you go around killing wolves?"

"I don't," Denny protested. "At least not that I know of."

Leah stood over the wounded man. Wade jerked his head. "You're in my light," he said.

She scooted back. "Sorry."

Wade bandaged the entry wound on his back which was much more compact than the exit wound on his front side, just under his ribs. "You were lucky, man. Could've done all kinds of damage."

"He was aiming to kill, I'm sure," Denny groused. "Bastard has a few screws loose these days."

"Is that so?" Leah had moved so she wouldn't impede Wade's work with the sutures. "Can't count on anyone these days."

"Listen. I'm not a bad guy. Tyson neither. We're out here because it's easy money. We come out and tranq a few wolves. Chuck takes them to a facility." He gasped as Wade put in another stitch. "For research."

Leah snorted. "No credible researcher approves of killing wolves," she said. "You did that."

"How do you know?" He jerked around to Wade. "How can she know that?"

Wade was too focused on his effort to patch up Denny to engage in the conversation.

"What I know and how isn't the point."

"Look, it wasn't…intentional," Denny said through clenched teeth. "We only fire live rounds at the wolves when protection is necessary."

Leah grunted, clearly unconvinced. "Tell me more about how all of this works."

"Chuck calls, we show up and do what he says."

"Even when he tells you to give a wolf or dog or whatever to another person?"

"That's all this is," Denny insisted. "Transport." He hissed a breath through his teeth. "That's all I do. I mean it," he added. "But this time, he's nuts. H-he…" His voice faded to a shuddering breath.

"He murdered Tyson last night," Leah said. "Is that what you can't spit out?"

"How?" Denny's wild gaze darted between Wade and Leah and back again. "How?"

"We were there," Leah said, kneeling close to Denny's face. "We saw it and you're going to turn yourself in."

"We were there," Wade repeated. "I did check after you buried him in the snow, but it was too late to help."

"Oh my God." Tears leaked from Denny's eyes. "He was a good friend. Loved to horse around."

As eulogies went, Wade thought that might be the best Tyson could ask for. He finished the sutures and covered the bullet wound with a gauze pad. "Easy now," he said, helping Wade sit up.

Leah dropped to one knee to look Denny in the eye. "Where is Chuck taking the wolves?"

"I don't know. The breeder."

"I want names," Leah demanded.

Denny sagged. "Chuck has all the information. He doesn't share details like that. I was taking the ATV to the first meeting point for next time."

Leah swore. Wade rested a hand on her shoulder, fearing she'd go on the attack and undo his repair job. "How about Denny takes the ATV back to West Yellowstone and turns himself in. He can share whatever he does know with the sheriff."

"Yes, I'll do that," Denny brightened. "I promise I'll go and report Tyson's murder. I'll tell them everything."

Wade didn't need to read minds to know Leah had zero faith in Denny's promises. She was glaring daggers at the guy. Still, it was the best option. They couldn't keep Denny with them, the risk was too high that he'd go on the attack given an opening.

He helped Denny to his feet, got the ATV righted and gave the guy a bottle of water and a few meal bars. "We'll notify the authorities that you're coming in," he said. "Don't let me down."

"I won't. I swear I won't," Denny vowed. "Whatever happens to me, I owe it to Tyson to go tell the truth."

LEAH WATCHED DENNY DRIVE AWAY. "You saved his life," she said. "I hope he doesn't waste his second chance."

Wade's field skills were a marvel. She admired the grit and perseverance he'd applied to turn a tragic loss into search and rescue expertise. Seeing him in action made her warm all over. She wanted to hug him, tell him how awesome he was. And then slug him for helping a man who had been hurting wolves.

He was remarkable, truly. And he was out here helping her. It gave her waning hope a vital boost.

Wade shrugged. "I hope he follows through. This situation could use a whistleblower."

She couldn't agree more, especially after the murder last night. "Think he'll actually turn himself in?"

Wade shaded his eyes with a hand, a scowl on his brow as the ATV disappeared over a rise. "Fifty-fifty," he said. "Assuming he doesn't pass out from the injury or run into a bison. You ready to move out?"

"Let me send an update." She fished the cell phone out of her inner pocket. "It'll give the research assistant a better chance of tracking Denny if he bolts."

"I tagged his ATV as well," Wade said with a wink. "We won't lose him."

The cell signal was strong enough that Leah made a call rather than send a text. Within a few minutes, they were back on Chuck's trail. They skirted around a herd of bison in their shaggy, snow-dotted coats and Leah couldn't resist taking several pictures. Mule deer tramped through a snowy meadow and she spotted a bobcat loping at the edge of the trees.

All of it made for a pristine winter wilderness she would miss terribly when her case here was closed.

The wind kicked up and she huddled a little closer to Wade as the afternoon sun gave way to evening. Behind them, the sun dropped closer to the horizon and Leah feared they were destined for another night in the tent. Not a thrilling prospect, despite the distinct appeal of snuggling close to Wade to stay warm. When he stopped for a radio check-in with his brother, she tried to search the park lodging app for a more substantial shelter.

Not far to the north, she saw an icon for another park ranger station. Too bad there was no way to know how far that would take them from Chuck's route. She didn't expect that he'd drive through the night, they couldn't afford to let him get too far ahead of them.

"You ready?" Wade asked, climbing back onto the ATV.

"I wish we had a drone," she grumbled, taking her seat behind him.

"Why?"

"It would be nice to see if there's any sign of a possible destination."

His lips tilted into a smile. "I'll add it to the supply list for next time." Adjusting his balaclava, he started the ATV and they were off again.

Her thoughts drifted as they bounced along, concerned about what they'd found so far. Would Denny keep his word and turn himself in, or would they be hunting for him later? She couldn't dwell on that. Her focus had to be on the safe recovery of those wolves and stopping the breeder exploiting the animals.

CHAPTER 9

WADE KEPT DRIVING, following the signal from the tracker on the truck. The vehicle had stopped about an hour ago. They had to be getting close. He'd no sooner thought it than Leah tugged on his coat. "We're about a half mile away," she said.

"All right. Let's walk from here."

Together, they tucked the ATV out of sight and hiked through the trees and over rough, snowy terrain, toward the blinking marker on the screen. They paused frequently to listen and assess the situation. The stillness set his teeth on edge. "Must've cut the engine," he said.

"There's the truck," Leah whispered as she pointed. "Tire is flat."

"About time something breaks our way."

She pulled out her binoculars. "Looks abandoned. No one's around."

"Wishful thinking," Wade countered. "Wolves are there, so Chuck has to be close. That must be the road Denny mentioned. Crowded by trees, but has to be the place."

"This location isn't saved on Ronnie's GPS."

"Ronnie was probably never cleared to come out here on his own. He was muscle for the captures, that's all." Wade studied the area, searching for any signs of a security system.

"If this is the breeding facility, it's practically right under the park service's nose," Leah mused. "The app shows a park ranger station not far from here."

"Probably out of service. They do that from time to time."

"Hmm. I guess that makes sense." She lowered the binoculars to look at him. "We need to get closer."

"Agreed."

Wade turned and lost himself in her dark brown eyes. He needed to focus on the job at hand, but for a moment he let himself get lost in the hot memory of their kisses. Just thinking back took the chill out of his blood. Her taste, the heat and silk of her lips, the rasp of her tongue dueling with his. He wanted her in ways he'd never thought possible. She dominated his thoughts, even out here facing the unknown. He wanted more than her safety, more than a solved case. He wanted her happiness, to see that sparkle in her eyes.

The biggest shock of all? He damn well wanted to be the man to make her happy for the rest of his days.

It was never supposed to be like this for him. How long had he avoided getting involved with anyone who could be hurt, possibly devastated, if he didn't come home from a mission? The last time he spoke with his mother, she reminded him she'd do it all over again. Fall in love, build a life and a partnership. That even losing her husband early, every single day had been worth it.

Whenever he looked at Leah, he caught a glimmer of what his mother must have meant. That strange blend of excitement and peace. Of knowing. But she'd been through so much and survived with such grace and strength. Not just out here, but back in vet school. Losing that dream had hurt her deeply. Maybe, having built such thick walls for his own protection, he could more easily see the similar walls Leah used to keep the world at a safe distance.

She wriggled backward. "What's the best approach?"

"I'm thinking," Wade said.

"You're scowling." But her eyes gleamed with amusement as she touched the furrow between his eyebrows.

Something not exactly unpleasant shifted in his gut. Affection or something more serious? Those answers had to wait.

"Same thing," he muttered.

Wade checked the area through the binoculars again. "Hell of a spot," he observed. They were out in the boonies and from this direction, he couldn't see a clearing big enough to land a helicopter. "We need to try and do a circuit without being noticed."

Going in without a backup solution wasn't acceptable. Guardian Agency protector or not, he refused to subject her to any more danger than necessary. His instincts were prickling. "I don't like this. Something feels off."

Down on the road, the caged wolves launched another vocal protest from the truck bed.

"Sounds like they agree with you," Leah said.

A moment later, different wolves replied. "Wade." She gripped his arm, her face alight with a mix of excitement and temper. "This must be the place. We found it! Those calls are coming from that direction."

He caught her before she could jump to her feet and reveal their hiding place to anyone who might be watching. "Hang tight. We have to assume there are cameras aimed toward the perimeter."

"Right." She sucked in a deep breath. "You're right."

He checked their position and the time. "Follow

my lead," Wade said, taking a path parallel to the long driveway. "Any conversation will wait until we're done."

She nodded.

His questions about the breeders pulling the strings on this operation continued to multiply. What leverage did they have on Chuck to keep him moving through impossible terrain and committing murder to protect their secrets?

Wade and Leah had proven themselves a credible threat, tracking the team so persistently. Anyone with common sense would have surrendered the wolves and walked away. Yet Chuck kept pressing on. To get here.

Within ten minutes, a rather rundown cabin came into view. The metal roof was mostly covered with snow and a thin plume of smoke rose from the chimney in the center of the building. At first glance, the building seemed to slump to one side, an effect of a deep snowdrift and a broken rail on the front porch. Based on the undisturbed snow on the porch and front steps, whoever lived in the cabin didn't use the front door at all.

Moving on, Wade kept an eye out for trail cameras, guards, or fencing. The big gaps in security were appalling considering the money involved in the operation.

On the other side of the cabin, the steps were clear, the snow pushed to either side. A path had been worn through the snow and Wade kept an eye on it as they continued to circle the property.

Hearing a shout, they dropped low, staying out of sight. A deep voice answered the first. Beside him, Leah tensed as Chuck appeared, talking with another man. Though they were too far away to hear the actual conversation, it was clear that Chuck was requesting help for the disabled truck in the drive.

A woman excitedly jogged out of a long metal building to join the two men. Ages and descriptions were impossible to determine with everyone bundled up for the elements. The three of them piled into a big truck and headed off.

Wade and Leah hunkered down, waiting for any further signs of people. He indicated she should wait where she was while he scooted down the hill to the long building. He crept around the cameras he could see and, as he suspected from the noises inside, discovered the building was being used as a kennel.

He was glad Leah wasn't here to see the animals penned up. Even he could recognize the longing to run free in the wild eyes of the captive animals. To his eye, the fencing dividing the pens didn't look as sturdy as it should.

Returning to Leah, he ushered her away as quickly as possible. "We're in the right place," he murmured as they traipsed away from the property. "Now we need to find a clearing Justice can use. Then we'll notify Stone."

Heading back toward the ATV, they found a clearing that would suffice. Satisfied they could come up with a workable solution, he pulled out the radio and called Stone.

"I'm glad to hear your voice," Stone said. "You missed your last check-in."

"Sorry about that," he replied. "We were doing some recon."

"Good. You should know that a guy named Denny showed up at the sheriff's station around noon today. He turned himself in for a variety of crimes ranging from poaching to murder."

Wade and Leah stared at each other. "I really thought he'd just keep running," Wade said to her.

"Guess he was sincere about being Tyson's friend," Leah reminded him.

"He tells us you patched him up," Stone continued.

"That's right," Wade said. "Things turned ugly with the latest capture. He's probably glad to be out of the thick of it. We found the illegal breeding site. Kennels and all." He caught Leah's hand. "I went in alone and saw several wolves and what I'm guessing are several more hybrids."

"You're there?" Stone's voice went straight into military operator mode. "Did you take pictures?"

"Yes. Basic recon complete," Wade reported.

"No pictures yet. We need to drop a net over this place before they get spooked and relocate."

Leah's tension was palpable and he was well-aware that she wasn't leaving without taking direct action.

"Agreed," Stone said. "How many personnel did you see on site?"

"Three," Wade and Lean answered together. "Leader of the ambush crew, male. One male and one female. I assume they live here."

"Weapons or patrols?"

"No patrols." A fact Wade considered short-sighted, even with the remote location. "No sign of heavy weapons. So far, we've encountered a shotgun, rifle, and handguns on the chase. A couple of trail cameras are posted near the kennel, but that's it. Several wolves and hybrids in a kennel building. One road in, currently blocked by a disabled truck."

"That won't last long." Leah murmured.

"You sure they don't know you're there?" Stone queried.

"If they do, they don't care," Wade replied. With the money on the line and the amount of effort Chuck had put in to deliver the wolves, if Wade and Leah had been seen, they would've drawn a reaction by now.

"Pull back to a safe location," Stone directed.

Beside him Leah bristled, lips parted and an argument sparking in her eyes. He gripped her hand. "Be patient for me," he murmured for her ears only. "One more time."

Her mouth firmed and she nodded.

"First light," Stone decided after a quiet moment. "We'll get support in place for you and have a team standing by for the animals."

Wade watched Leah take a deep breath.

"We'll go at first light," Wade confirmed. Beside him, Leah glared.

And she called him the scowly one.

LEAH BARELY KEPT her complaints locked down as they drove the ATV away from the breeder's sketchy compound. Surely going in at night would be better. Cover of darkness and all of that. They were technically outnumbered and—

"Stop it," Wade scolded as they entered the shuttered ranger station.

"Stop what?"

He pulled off his gloves and touched her forehead, smoothing the space between her eyebrows. "Thinking of arguments."

"I'm not."

He cocked his head.

She yanked off her own gloves. "Fine. I am." She unwound her scarf and started undoing her coat. "We're so close. If we lose them now…" Words failed her as potential disappointment loomed large in her mind.

"We won't. It's a matter of hours, that's all."

And just like that, she was at ease in his assurances. His ability to do that should irritate her. It didn't. For whatever reason, when Wade applied that confident calm, she wanted to revel in it, savor the peace of mind he offered.

"You're right." She sighed. He wasn't going to let the breeder slip away, as committed now as she'd been from the start. "They really didn't seem to know we were there."

Wade shrugged out of his coat and helped her do the same. "And I doubt Chuck will mention us."

That stumped her. "How does he explain arriving alone?"

Wade moved through the doorway to the compact central room that served as den and bedroom. A worn loveseat and chair faced the fireplace and a daybed was tucked into the corner. He knelt by the hearth and opened the flue. With the available supplies, he quickly got a fire going.

"Chuck clearly calls the shots out here," Wade said. "If the breeder team is deep into the work, would they care much about how the transport gets done?"

"Probably not as long as the money is flowing in." A chill slid through her system, the now-familiar reaction to people doing bad things for lousy reasons. "That's the one downside of my work," she confessed with a shiver.

He rubbed his hands up and down her arms in a casual, automatic effort to warm her up. "One downside?" He made it sound like there should be several. He tipped up her chin, his burning gaze holding her captive. "Oh. You mean seeing people at their worst."

"That's the one," she managed.

Breathless, nearly frozen, and somehow Wade made all that fade away. Little jolts of heat flashed through her system. The fragrance of snow and pine swirled around her, clung to their skin, but the undercurrent of his masculine scent stirred her. Need and desire and something she wasn't sure she'd ever be willing to give again bloomed inside her.

Trust.

"Wade..." She didn't know quite how to ask for what she needed from him. Wasn't sure she could explain what she was offering. More than a little desperate, she let her body lead. Pushing up on her toes, she touched her mouth to his. Lightning struck again, and the kiss went from sweet temptation to an all-consuming blaze in an instant.

He wrapped her in his arms, pulling her hard against his chest. Running her hands over his shoulders, she explored the firm muscles under his clothing, then started shoving the fabrics out of her way.

His taste was addictive. The bold strokes of his tongue fueled the fire in her belly. She needed to see him, to feel his skin on hers. To have other parts of him stroking into her body.

She needed to give herself this moment. Take a leap. With Wade. He wouldn't let her down. Wouldn't use her or betray her.

His hands slid under her sweater and the thermal, slowly, slowly tracing her ribs before cupping her breasts. "Wade." His name was her only coherent thought.

"Talk to me," he urged, trailing kisses up and down her neck. "Tell me what you want."

"You." She forced her eyes open, determined to leave no room for doubt between them. The fierce hunger in his brown eyes made her knees weak. He caught her, his lips tilting into an irresistible half-smile. "You," she repeated.

"I'm yours." He pulled off her layers of shirts and bent his head to nuzzle her breasts through her bra. "All yours, Leah."

She shoved off his flannel and the thermal underneath, sighing when, at last, she could lay her hands on his sculpted chest. His moan echoed hers and he covered her hands with his own. Then he boosted her into his arms. She wrapped her legs around his waist and her hips naturally flexed into the ridge of his erection. Felt so good, she could come from that alone.

He swore softly. His hands squeezed her butt, stilling her movements and holding her close to the heat of him.

"One second."

Setting her back on her feet, he kept her close as he rooted into one of the supply packs. Pulling out a box of condoms, the grin on his face was full of wicked promises.

"Justice?" She laughed.

"Who else? I'm sure it was a joke."

"A timely one," she said. "Remind me to thank your brother later."

"Much later." His voice was growly and the shiver that skated over her skin was all about anticipation.

He captured her lips, kissing her as he guided her toward the fireplace. He paused long enough to drag the mattress off the daybed in front of the hearth while she followed with the quilt and blankets.

He tossed the condoms down and dropped to his knees to finish undressing her. As he stared up at her, she felt treasured rather than exposed. "You're falling behind," she teased, tracing the ridges of his muscular shoulders.

"Not for long." He dispensed with the rest of his clothing and drew her down with him, covering her with his body. "Warm enough?"

Her heart melted at the sincere concern in his gaze. No one had ever looked at her that way. But feeling his erection pressing against her thigh, the taut, fascinating strength of him from head to toe, all she could do was give him a nod. A smile. And bring his mouth to hers for another sizzling kiss.

Soon his kisses were trailing lower, closing hot and insistent over her breast. She gasped as the pleasure jolted through her. He suckled, tugging lightly on her nipple with his teeth. She shuddered, her fingers diving through his thick hair.

"Wade," she panted. Her hips rocked and her fingers curled around his arms, urging him up and close. She couldn't get close enough. "Wade, I need you. Now."

"Patience, darling." He took her mouth with such a tender kiss, tears threatened.

Patience was beyond her. Her body was already quaking, perched on the edge of an orgasm she wanted more than her next breath.

His hands seemed to be everywhere, featherlight one second, bold and sure the next. With his mouth on hers, he stroked her belly and down over her thighs until they fell open. She moaned as his fingers slipped through her wet folds, delving inside her and then gliding up to her clitoris.

She grabbed his strong wrist, seeking a respite, desperate to catch her breath, but it was too late.

The next flick of his fingers sent her flying apart, her body shivering in delight. "Wade." Her craving for him outweighed her embarrassment over her lightning-quick response to him. She'd hardly made a secret of wanting him.

The scruff of his whiskers added to her shivers as he kissed a pathway down her body, moving over her and shouldering her thighs apart. "Wade. Oh." Her breath caught. "You can't be serious."

"I'm serious all right." He blew softly over her sensitive flesh.

"Wade." She covered her face with her hands. Being laid bare, literally, was challenging enough. But suddenly she realized her heart was just as vulnerable. The abrupt awareness hit her with unexpected force. Overwhelmed, she squirmed beneath him. "It's too much."

"Not even close." His tongue lapped at her. "Come on, sweetheart. One more time."

His mouth and hands coaxed and teased, until every nerve was on edge, and every thought of him alone. The world, right now, was no bigger than the two of them in this lumpy bed. She didn't want to be anywhere else.

Didn't want any other man with her.

Only Wade.

She cried out his name, chasing that pure sensual rush of another orgasm. He rose over her, grabbed a condom from the box and rolled it over his straining erection and then—finally—he filled her with one long, perfect thrust.

They moved in a sinuous rhythm that was all heat and joy and amazing sensation. She felt more connected than she'd known a person could be. It went beyond the delicious physical contact of his solid muscles and blazing skin under her hands. Her pulse and breath matched and blended with his, until she was no longer sure where her body stopped and his began.

Pleasure and need twined together, tighter and tighter, driving her toward another climax. This time, as her body clutched and trembled, as she called out his name, he found his release as well.

For a long moment, Wade rested on top of her, a lovely satisfying weight as his lips toyed with the shell of her ear. Then he rolled away to dispose of the condom, covering her with the quilt and blankets.

When he returned, he brought along the pillows and slid under the covers, drawing her close until she was sprawled over his chest, her legs tangled with his.

"Mm. That's perfect," he crooned, wrapping his arms around her.

She agreed, snuggling into his embrace. Nothing had ever been so fabulous as wallowing in the afterglow, happiness coursing through her system from her head to her toes. This light and fizzy feeling was almost too perfect. It would be so easy to call it love, to give him the words that hovered on her lips. She muted herself in the nick of time, pressing kisses to his skin.

Too soon. Way too soon for any declarations beyond amazing sex.

His hands roamed up and down her back. She sighed under the tender caresses. In love with Wade. She liked the way that felt all over, inside and out. He was smart and kind and sexy as hell. And he didn't dismiss her ideas or drive. She'd found it rather remarkable that he'd been indignant, even before he'd heard the whole story, about the situation that booted her out of vet school.

Wonderful as they were, these few hours were fleeting. Had to be. This one night, a brief interlude that ranked as the best of her life, was probably it. Not because she was afraid of the ruthless breeder, but because they were sure to go their separate ways when this was done.

Still, the memories would last a lifetime. She'd carry this moment with Wade long after she left West Yellowstone.

WADE HELD his breath as he scooted out from under Leah's warm body. He tucked the blankets around her to keep her cozy. He didn't want her to ever be cold again. Not an easy feat in this part of the world. Maybe she'd join him on a tropical vacation when this was over.

She curled into the pillow with a soft sigh and suddenly he was questioning all of his choices. With Leah it was harder to retain his resolve to prevent heartache. He worked in a dangerous career and he didn't want her waiting up, worrying.

Except he sure liked the idea of coming in from a job and sinking into her arms. Her body. Talking through the process of a rescue—or anything else.

He tried to put a cap on this sudden surge of emotion. He couldn't be in love with her, but he sure sounded like Justice raving about Payton weeks ago.

Building a life with a lover had never been part of Wade's plan. Still wasn't.

Until Leah.

He simultaneously wanted to wake her up and talk about it and let her sleep until the last possible minute. Maybe longer. He hurried to the cold bathroom to get cleaned up and clear his head.

Soon they would be hiking back to the breeding site. Unless... He could call Stone. If the team handled the raid, gathering up the breeder and recovering the animals, Wade could get Leah back home. Keep her safe. The more he thought about it, the more he liked the idea. That's why they were here, why they'd joined Brotherhood Protectors in the first place: search and rescue, protect and save. Could he pitch it so she would understand?

"Want some company?" Leah pulled back the shower curtain and stepped in with him before he could answer.

And for the next several minutes, he forgot everything but the fantastic pleasure of having her body close to his. He couldn't wait to bury himself to the hilt in her again. Just as soon as they were done with this damned illegal breeder. As they toweled off, he realized he couldn't possibly deny her a part in the takedown. She'd been on the case too long not to see it through.

At least the decision saved him from trying to find a private moment to make the call. There were challenges ahead today for sure, but he would find a way to keep her safe through the most difficult test yet.

LIGHT WASN'T MORE than a faint wish on the horizon when they returned to the breeder's run-down facility. Wade wrestled with the litany in his head, telling him to keep Leah out of harm's way. As if she would've let him leave the ranger station without her. She was set on seeing this through.

He couldn't blame her, but capable and determined might not be enough to wrap this up. He shook off the doubts gripping the back of his neck and blamed the icy sensation between his shoulder blades on the bitterly cold weather.

Negativity never got the job done.

They'd gone over the plan. Spoken with Stone and Justice. And reviewed a few contingencies. Nothing left but to do the job they were here to do.

"If I tell you to run, you run," he murmured as they huddled in the shadows of the trees.

"No," she replied in a whisper.

He turned swiftly, catching her face between his gloved hands. "This isn't a negotiation, Leah. We have different training. Let me call the shots out here."

"Sure. I understand that." She yanked down her scarf and pressed her lips to his. "I'll follow any order except the one to leave you behind."

"Leah."

She smothered his protest with another hot, fast kiss. "Wade. We've got this."

Where was all this confidence coming from? He gazed into her big brown eyes and felt some of the worry lift away. With Leah, it felt as if the belief was contagious. They could do this. They had the element of surprise and the advantage of a deep commitment to something bigger than a payday.

He was stalling. They had fresh batteries in the radios and the team had the coordinates. He didn't have to call to know they were standing by. Chelsea was set, more eager than Leah to get the animals back to the research center once Wade and Leah gave the all clear. In a matter of hours, this would be over and done.

They weren't infiltrating a terrorist bunker with soldiers armed to the teeth. This wasn't a natural disaster, though Leah would vehemently argue against that assessment. It made him smile to think of it. The woman was a force. One that wouldn't give up now that she had the target in view. Plus, his team was ready to leap into the fray if necessary. Justice was probably more than halfway through his pre-flight checklist already.

"Give me your word," he insisted. "I'm not letting you tag along if you're hell-bent on taking unnecessary risks."

"Tag along?" she echoed. "For your sake, I'll forget you said that. I do promise to listen." She swiped an 'x' over her heart. "Let's go."

She started moving toward the barn before he could say anything else. Before he could tell her he was in love with her and would walk through any blizzard or blaze to keep her safe today and every day to come.

With all of that on his mind, it was probably for the best that she was out of reach and definitely out of earshot.

Watching Leah scan the area, he realized reason and logic weren't going to help him get over her. Body and soul, he wanted her. His heart longed to know if she felt the same way.

Her passion for her work was clear. She might view all of this as a matter of protection or gathering evidence for a legal case against the breeder, but she cared about these animals and their environment as a whole.

His stomach twisted. Could she possibly care about him? With an effort he shifted his focus to the task at hand. Distraction wouldn't help any more than negativity. When they were done here, he could ask her outright what it would take to keep her in West Yellowstone.

To keep her with him.

For now, he let her lead as they crept along, sticking to the shadows. The truck was gone. Wade hoped they hadn't lost Chuck or the wolves he'd captured. Moving parallel to the rutted path that served as a driveway, Wade stepped in front of her as soon as the buildings came into view.

"I'll draw their attention. You move into that main building."

She nodded.

"Shoot first if you're threatened," he reminded her, fighting the urge to change the plan to keep her in sight. "Don't let anyone talk you into being vulnerable."

Her eyes went wide and her body trembled. "Not my first dance with a bad guy," she said. "Let's move before they realize we're here."

There was no reason to think they'd been led into a trap and yet the idea plagued Wade as they split up. Leah headed for the boxy little house as he moved toward the long kennel building.

The light over the door was still lit and a thin line of smoke rose from the lone, central chimney, but the windows were dark. Wade darted across the open area, telling himself she'd be fine as soon as he drew everyone to him.

Gunfire—a shotgun—blasted, shattering the stillness of the morning.

Wade threw himself around the corner, knocking his shoulder into the corrugated paneling of the building. The wolves and hybrids inside reacted accordingly. Fine by him. He wanted as much noise as possible.

Rolling to his knees, he took stock of where he was and where the shooter must've been. And saw the truck.

"You're mine now!" Chuck's bellow only stirred up the wolves just as they were quieting down. "Come quietly and I'll let you live," he shouted.

As if Wade believed that. Chuck had already killed one man, though he probably didn't realize he'd been seen.

"You're out of your league, cowboy."

Wade edged closer to the door, timing his movements to the barks and yips of the annoyed wolves. He slapped at the siding, earned another noisy chorus from the wolves and hybrids inside, and then rounded the next corner. He fumbled the sliding bolt, managing to duck inside just before Chuck fired again.

Buckshot rang out against the metal siding, a harsh descant to the agitated animals inside. Wade was sure he'd miscalculated as a large gray wolf in the nearest pen sized him up. Just like yesterday, Wade had his doubts that the fencing would hold. From a quick scan, it appeared that none of the animals had been moved out.

One positive. Now to create a diversion that would give Leah a chance to search the house.

Ignoring the low, menacing growls, he waited for Chuck to follow him inside, well-aware the man wouldn't want to threaten a big payoff by firing his shotgun in here.

Melting snow dripped and trickled through the leaky roof, puddling in the central aisle.

Chuck shoved through the door with the shotgun looped across his back and a big hunting knife in his hands. He reached out and hit the switch for the overhead lights, putting his back to Wade.

It was the opening he needed and he attacked.

LEAH WAS WATCHING the back door of the house when the gunshot startled her. Her heart leaped into her throat, lodging there. Had a guard gone unnoticed during their recon? That was the best possible outcome, considering the alternative was Chuck working to kill Wade.

She locked down the worry that bathed her skin in a sudden, cold sweat. Wade could handle himself. More importantly, he was counting on her to handle this part of the takedown. She needed to go in and find any documentation possible to connect the dots between breeders and buyers.

Another gunshot nearly undid her. She braced against the trunk of a tree and closed her eyes. She would not let Wade down.

In the kennel, the animals were in a tizzy, the vocalizations growing louder. It wasn't the expected signal but it was likely enough to draw out the other two people they'd seen last night.

Lights came on at one end of the cabin and Leah crouched down, sinking deeper into the shadows, waiting. The man they'd seen during yesterday's recon threw open the back door and hollered at Chuck through the radio.

Chuck didn't respond.

On an irritable oath, the man stomped into a pair of boots and bundled into a coat as he started toward the kennel.

"Rex, wait for me!" a woman called from inside the house.

A name at last, Leah thought, making a mental note.

"Stay here," he shouted over his shoulder. "I'll find Chuck and let you know what the hell is going on."

The woman hesitated in the open doorway, watching Rex lumber across the snow. Finally, she retreated and closed the door on the cold morning. More light filled the windows as the woman moved around.

Leah hadn't heard the click of a lock. Most likely the door was open. "No time like the present," she whispered. Picking up a short limb from the snowy ground she moved up to the door as quietly as possible. Best if she didn't have to use the gun at all.

She tested the doorknob, relieved when it turned easily. With the improvised weapon raised and ready, she nudged open the door. It swung back toward her, hard, but Leah blocked it with the limb.

"Get the hell off my property!" the woman shouted, struggling against Leah. "Rex! Rex! Someone is breaking in."

Leah hit the door with her shoulder and wedged more of her body in, widening the gap. She fell awkwardly in the scrum, but managed to get inside, kicking the door shut.

The woman fell on top of her and Leah was stuck defending herself, protecting her eyes and face from a flurry of blows from a fist and the radio. She bucked her hips and gained a quick advantage. She squeezed her knees tight into the woman's ribs, cutting off her air.

"Stop," Leah ordered. "I don't want to hurt you."

The woman spit and swore until Leah shoved

her coat-covered arm into the woman's mouth. "Listen to me. Your illegal breeding is over. Settle down."

The woman subsided, but Leah wasn't fooled. She eased up, just enough to grab the cord she had in her pocket and quickly restrained the woman's hands. She wriggled down to secure her legs as well, despite the woman's writhing. After Leah locked the door, she pulled the woman up enough to lean on the battered couch, a safe distance from any possible weapon.

"Who the hell are you?" the woman demanded. "You have no right to intrude on Dr. Wallace's ongoing work. This is a gray wolf research outpost."

The language, the implication that the woman thought she was here for a legitimate cause, pulled Leah up short. "Funded by?"

"A federal grant. The name wouldn't mean anything to you. I've been the lead assistant for over a year."

Leah laughed at the absurdity. "What's your name?" She glanced around, looking for a computer. No way they handled all of the DNA and documentation out in the kennel. "How did you get selected?"

"Millie Greer. It was a conference presentation and the standard application and interview process."

Not a chance. "Let me guess." Leah folded her arms over her chest and stared down at Millie. "It took about six months for an interview." Millie gaped. "You don't have a husband, kids or any other family connections." Now Millie's pale eyebrows snapped into a frown. "Dr. Wallace required a rigorous background check and warned you there would be limited connectivity or contact with outsiders."

"Yes," Millie said, frowning. "H-how do you know all of that?"

"Classic isolation techniques. You're more likely to be dedicated and loyal and gullible without outside obligation or influence." She was starting to feel sorry for Millie when she caught a calculating glint in the woman's eyes and reconsidered. "Makes the real work he's been doing out here easier. Do you know what happens to the animals when they leave here?"

Millie opened her mouth and more gunfire sounded. This time it sounded like two different weapons and much closer to the house.

"How much do you know, Millie?" Leah demanded.

"Nothing. Dr. Rex Wallace has the connections. We share data and lineage with other researchers," Millie said. "I don't know any names." Tears glistened in her eyes. "We sometimes exchange animals."

Leah wasn't buying the innocent act. "Chuck does the hauling?"

"Sometimes," Millie replied. Her shoulders slumped as if she was defeated.

"Cozy little place," Leah said. "Where do you work?"

Millie curled her lip in a decent imitation of a snarling animal. "Out in the kennels."

"Fine. Play stupid. You'll probably look good in prison stripes." Keeping an eye on Millie, Leah used her radio to report the names she had and the status of the takedown. Stone would share the information with the Guardian Agency.

She backed up and peeked around the corner and discovered the kitchen had been adjusted to have a workstation on one end. Three laptops and two large monitors dominated a long table. A radio scanner occupied a small table in the corner. She turned that off out of spite. Paperwork was scattered across every flat surface and there was a filing cabinet under the table, between the two chairs. Millie shouted dire threats, but it was the rise of male voices outside the kitchen door that pushed Leah into action.

Using the cell phone, she took several pictures, first of the space in general, then of individual papers lying about. Millie shouted. Wood splintered. But Leah was consumed with the log book that showed Chuck's schedule for the past year.

Handwritten in an accounting notebook, the lettering was precise. And it matched the notes around the workstation with a ceramic mug stained with pink lipstick. Millie was up to her eyeballs in the worst parts of Wallace's operation.

She took more pictures and hit send, just as the back door burst open and Wade and Dr. Wallace tumbled in.

CHAPTER 11

WADE'S first thought as he landed hard on top of the man Chuck had called Doc, was that Leah wasn't hurt. She looked fine. Healthy. And rather angelic with the light filtering around her from her vantage point in a doorway.

Her mouth had dropped open and her eyes were wide, but she wasn't the woman screaming at him. Or maybe the woman was berating Doc.

Didn't really matter.

Wade had managed to lock Chuck into an open kennel before Doc had stormed into the building. Wade was covered in mud from the fight that followed. No surprise Doc fought dirty. Wade didn't care. He'd do whatever was necessary to see this through for Leah. And the wolves.

Unfortunately, Doc was also a sneaky and slippery fighter. Desperate even. They'd scrambled and wrestled their way back to the cabin.

"Make the call!" Wade pitched his voice over the shouting between Doc and the woman.

He didn't have a chance to say anything else as Doc wriggled enough and stiff-armed Wade's jaw. Wade countered, leveraging away and using two quick moves to break the older man's arm. Doc howled in pain, the woman started weeping and through it all, he thought he heard Leah calling in the team.

With Leah's help, he secured Doc's feet and made sure neither of the breeders could escape. Then he slumped to his back, staring at the planked wood ceiling of the cabin. "This didn't go at all as planned."

"But we got it done," Leah said.

"Hope you're right." It was either the steady beat of the helicopter rotor or just his pulse pounding in his ears. Probably his pulse. It was too soon for the helo, even with Justice at the controls.

Leah's gorgeous face hovered over him. "It's safe," she said, crouching at his side.

"I'm sore all over," he confessed, managing to sit up. "Chuck's locked in with the wolves," he said. "He tried to unlock a few of the gates, but all the animals are accounted for."

"You'll pay for this!" Millie was shouting again. In the small cabin, her shrill voice was more than unpleasant. "Trespassing and assault are just the beginning."

"The woman could talk paint off a wall." Leah gave his shoulder a squeeze. "Be right back."

He watched, more than a little in awe as Leah grabbed the back of Millie's shirt and dragged her through the door, down the rickety steps and shoved her into a pile of snow. The least he could do was help her with Doc.

"If I were you, I'd keep that arm in the snow. Reduce the inflammation," he said as the breeders complained.

"They were in this deep. For years," Leah said as they tramped back inside, leaving the door open to watch their captives. "She gave me a song and dance about her lack of knowledge, but it's her handwriting in these sales ledgers."

Wade whistled low.

"I've sent the initial information up the line. To your team and mine." Her voice broke on that last word.

He slid his arm around her shoulders, gave her a squeeze. "It's over. You did it."

"We did it." She sniffed. "I was about to dig into the breeding records when you and Wallace rolled in."

"Ha. Ha." He pulled her close, just let himself rest with her. "You're one hell of a hunter, Leah. Awesome instinct, grit, and determination."

"Millie wasn't so tough," she demurred. "You had the bigger challenge, taking down a killer."

He still hated that she'd seen it. Been that close to a greedy, murderous, bastard like Chuck. "If you want to walk down and see him in a cage—" The radio clipped to her belt crackled as Justice checked in, asking for a status report.

Leah stepped away to gather the breeding records and financials as Wade discussed the logistics of getting Wallace, Chuck, and Millie into custody.

A few minutes later, the sheriff, two deputies, Chelsea, and Bobby arrived. Wade filled in the details of the takedown with broad strokes and once Wallace and Millie were better secured, he escorted the group to the kennel. Chuck was still trying to break free, spewing threats and dire promises when he spotted Wade.

He pointed to Chuck. "That one has been working with Wallace for some time. And he's a killer," Wade warned the sheriff. "Leah found the breeding records," he explained to Chelsea and Bobby. "This way," he said, leading the wolf researchers further along the aisle, leaving the deputies to read Chuck his rights. "These are the four animals that were captured a few days ago."

"They all look healthier than I expected." Chelsea studied the set up. "They need space, but they aren't malnourished."

Wade left the researchers to deal with the animals, jogging back to the cabin to find Leah. She was his priority now. Finally, his only priority.

LEAH WATCHED Wade stoke the fire in the cabin's wood stove while they waited for Justice to return and pick them up from the breeding site. "Need another blanket?" he asked.

"No, thanks." Leah had tried to be productive, studying the records of sales and exchanges, but her eyes were tired and her vision was starting to blur.

"You should relax," Wade said.

"I know."

"All of this will be collected."

"I know," she repeated.

There had been a brief discussion about taking one of the breeder's trucks back across to West Yellowstone, but Leah didn't want to jeopardize any potential evidence. Plus, after what they'd been through, she wasn't sure either of them could stay awake on the journey.

Justice had suggested they wait here, in the cabin with a good fire, for his return.

She'd been too exhausted to argue.

"Come here," he wedged himself onto the lumpy couch, drawing her up against his side. "Relax," he suggested again, this time adding a kiss to the top of her head.

She sighed. "It's over."

"You did it," he agreed.

She closed her eyes and snuggled into the comfort he offered. But she was too weary to really sleep. "Wade?" she asked, watching the flames dance behind the black grate of the stove.

"Right here."

"I really love the outdoors," she said.

"I sense a "but" in there."

She tipped her head back so she could see his face. She loved his face. "But I'd really like a hot shower and a real bed. My bed."

"Not mine?" he teased. "That's rude."

She giggled, surprised it was even possible to laugh considering what they had endured. "Yours is at the lodge," she reminded him. "I'm done with temporary accommodations. At least for a while."

The fact was, she didn't recall much about the bed they'd shared, other than he'd been in it with her. Her cheeks went hot, along with the rest of her as she relived the fresh, sexy memories. For a precious few hours she hadn't thought about the plight of the wolves.

"It will be good to get home," he said.

The word might as well have been a bucket of ice water dousing her in a shocking reality. They were about to go home. She had an apartment in

West Yellowstone, of course. But it wasn't home for her. Not really. It was a temporary assignment.

Wade had made the move with his team. He would likely be looking for a permanent place now that he'd finished his mission to find her.

Although she cared deeply for Wade, feelings didn't change facts. Leah lived somewhat nomadically. She visited her parents for random weekends and holidays when it fit her protection schedule. Other than that, she went where the work carried her. That had always felt right.

She sat back, rubbing at the panic bubbling in her chest, squeezing her heart.

"You okay?" He tilted his head.

"I'm fine." Her attempt at a smile failed, based on the frown pinching his brow. "Really," she added, hoping to convince one of them.

What she and Wade had endured, the connection they'd found during their ordeal out here in the wilderness, might not hold up under the light of reality back in town. Making love with Wade hadn't been an exercise in survival, it had been deeper than that. But enough to build on? Enough to make another career shift? She just didn't know.

Would Wade be open to a long-distance relationship? Was she? All of this was probably irrelevant. Maybe the connection was simply due to the crisis and not something to hang her heart on.

She'd find out soon enough.

Scooting off the couch, she escaped to the kitchen for another bottle of water and a little space to think. She couldn't decide if it was regret or relief coursing through her that she'd kept her feelings locked down. Giving him an "I love you" in the heat of passion would have backfired and made everything more awkward.

More awkward than this. Because now she didn't know where those words could fit into any of the conversations they'd be likely to have in the immediate future.

Sheer willpower carried her back out to him and his thoughtful scowl. "Thank you for everything."

"Leah."

Whatever else he might've said was forgotten as they both heard the helicopter's return. "That's our ride." She held out her hand, needing to touch him. Especially if it was the last time she'd be this close.

At the helicopter, she saw relief and brotherly love on Wade's face. "We are glad to see you," he said.

Justice flipped up his sunglasses. "Done saving the wild world?"

"We are." Wade handed her into the helicopter. "Thanks for doing this."

"Hey, if you can't use your skills for family, why bother?"

"Thanks, Justice," Leah said.

"My pleasure. You'll find hand warmers in that box between the seats. Payton insisted. She sent coffee too." He handed the thermos to Wade as soon as they were buckled in.

She drank deeply when he offered her the cup. Didn't even care that the hot liquid scalded the tip of her tongue. "I'm going to burn these clothes when we get back," she said.

"Hey, I gave you those gloves," Wade joked.

"You did." She studied her gloved hands. "Thank you very much."

Her stomach dropped as the helicopter lifted off and she smiled at Wade. No, she wouldn't burn the gloves. They would stay with her, a permanent addition to the small collection of possessions that she took along for every assignment. She'd think of them as her good luck charm.

Without Wade, she wouldn't be alive.

Without Wade, she wouldn't have found the wolves or the illegal breeder.

And without Wade, she suspected she'd still be searching for that empowering and amazing emotion called love.

CHAPTER 12

WADE HAD BEEN in plenty of tight situations through the years. As a kid caught under that avalanche with his dad, during his military service, and during civilian rescue operations. This entire operation, from start to finish, was a thousand times different. Didn't require a degree in rocket science to figure out the variable.

Leah.

She'd been amazing in that crisis. And the smidge of time they'd had to themselves had only reinforced that what they'd found during their race to save the wolves was a true and marvelous connection.

When the helicopter arrived, he'd helped her in and buckled in beside her, grateful that they were done. Done with criminal behavior, done with the biting cold, and done—for a time—with the wolves.

No one would give Leah any more trouble today. Or ever, if he had a say in it.

He had more to think about than his own safety and welfare now. Working with trained partners and teammates might make a good career, but Leah's passion and courage for her cause had given him a new perspective.

Above and beyond all of that, she was the woman he loved.

A few days ago, he'd been sent into the wilderness to find a lost woman and instead he was returning to his team with so much more. His life had pulled a one-eighty on him. Again. This change felt as life-altering as the day he'd lost his dad, though the emotions rolling through him were on the happier side of the scale.

Wade thought he'd understood love. He hadn't known how loving someone specific created an entirely new definition of the word. Leah had changed everything. Hell, the way he breathed felt more significant. Deeper. Despite everything inside him feeling weak and wobbly and damned uncomfortable.

Grateful he could sit with his thoughts on the ride back to West Yellowstone, he was frustrated that he couldn't talk or touch Leah the way he wanted to. He kept reminding himself they were almost back to civilization where they could figure out what to do next. Together.

As much as Wade trusted Justice as a pilot and a brother, he'd never been happier for a helo to touch down. Wade shuddered under a wave of exhaustion.

Leah gave a start, concern shining in her gaze. "You okay?"

"Getting there," he said. "I feel like I lost a standoff with a steamroller. Or a grizzly." Just about every inch of him ached. Including his heart.

"Sounds about right." She squeezed his hand. "But we won."

"That we did." He leaned down to kiss her, but she shifted out of his reach, dropped his hand. "Leah." His personal questions were shoved aside as Stone pulled up in one of the team SUVs.

"Am I glad to see the two of you," he said, striding forward. "Justice kept us apprised, but I would've enjoyed getting my hands dirty on this one."

"It went down pretty fast," Leah said.

"We had everything we needed," Wade agreed. "Big help knowing everyone was on alert."

"Fair enough." Stone took a deep breath. "Plenty of people want the full report." He tipped his head back toward the vehicle. "We're set for you at the lodge. You'll have time to get cleaned up before we loop in everyone at the barn."

On the short drive back to the Brotherhood Protectors headquarters, Leah let Wade answer

Stone's immediate queries, all but fading into the shadows of the backseat. At the lodge, the distance only increased. After all they'd been through, Leah walked right by him to a different room to clean up and change clothes rather than stay with him.

Maybe she wasn't ready to publicly declare that they were a couple. Or maybe her feelings didn't match his own and he was being a pushy idiot about the whole thing. All he could do was deal with the necessities. Only then would the two of them have time to speak freely and privately.

Annoyed with himself and the circumstances, Wade showered off the grime from the wilderness trek. The clean jeans and thermal shirt smelled so good and felt even better. He grabbed a flannel and pulled on thick socks and warm boots, lacing them up in record time. Rushing into the hallway, he waited for Leah to reappear.

He suspected Chelsea or Kyla had brought toiletries and clean clothes from Leah's apartment. Assuming she'd let anyone close enough to have a spare key. Then again, both Chelsea and Kyla were bold, strong-willed, and more than capable of getting things done, with or without a key or the support of a landlord.

Whatever was going on in Leah's head, Wade wouldn't let her withdraw. Couldn't. After days of following the gang to the hybrid breeding ranch, he was hers. Body and soul. He had no idea what was next, but he didn't want to face a future without Leah in his life. All of his adult life he'd avoided the kind of ties that had grown between himself and Leah, determined not to become a source of grief for anyone.

Bad enough for his family if he screwed up and didn't come home; adding to the number of people who would miss him had seemed selfish. Foolish.

Yet, here he was, completely hooked and hoping to stay that way. A strange sensation squeezed his chest. He rubbed his sternum. What would he do, how awful would he feel if Leah didn't feel the same connection?

Waiting for her, he kept replaying how she'd drawn away from him in the past hours. As if the conversations, bonding, and incredible intimacy of their experience had all been an illusion.

One more debrief and then they could find some privacy and clear the air.

He checked his watch, fighting back a surge of unlikely worry that she'd left the lodge without him. Finally, the door opened. She looked incredible, her dark hair falling straight, spilling over a creamy cable-knit sweater. Dark jeans and worn brown boots completed her look. For a brief moment, her eyes flared with surprise when she saw him waiting.

Where else would he be? Why didn't she understand he was never going to let her face anything alone? Not if he had a choice in the matter.

"Ready?" he asked, ignoring that flicker of uncertainty. He held out a hand, unease dancing down his spine before she closed the distance and set her hand in his. She smelled incredible, like fresh apples. Though he hadn't minded the scent of campfire smoke, snow, and pine clinging to hair and skin when they'd made love.

He had her close for less than a minute before she stopped in the hallway, withdrawing her phone from her pocket. "It's a message from the research center," she said. "Sounds like the wolves are settled in. The team will be observing for a few days and the vets will make sure each animal looks right before taking them back to the pack rendezvous point."

"They just go ahead and release them and hope for the best?" he asked.

"Once they're deemed healthy, sure," she replied. "Chelsea knows what she's doing. She'll make sure those wolves have the best possible outcome."

"I'm glad to hear it. That's always the goal for search and rescue."

"Even wolf rescue?"

"Well, it's my first, but I'd say we did well." He held out a coat and Leah slid her arms into the sleeves. He stroked her shoulders lightly before stepping back. After so many hours fighting to stay warm, he didn't want her ever to feel chilled again.

A sense of pride washed over him and he took a deep breath of the crisp air as they walked down to the barn Stone had converted into a Brotherhood Protectors headquarters.

"I feel awesome," he confessed. "The five of us came out here to do what we do best and help people, but what we just accomplished was amazing. I never imagined anything like that."

"Wade." She came to a halt outside the barn door. "I, um." She shoved her hands into her pockets. "I never would've shut down that breeder without your help. I wouldn't have survived that second night." Her gaze on the sky overhead, she added. "I've been thinking about it nonstop since… since we turned over the gang to the sheriff."

"The sheriff wouldn't have known about any of it without you. Your research, your commitment got us there."

The wind caught at her hair and she shook the dark silk back from her face. "It wasn't just the elements or the breeder. You saved me from myself, Wade. I can't ever thank you enough."

Was this why she kept drawing away? Was it a misplaced gratitude issue? No, he couldn't let her think that's what was happening. The words were there, words he should've said earlier, before she got stuck in her own thoughts. "Leah, listen—"

Stone stepped out of the barn. "There you are. Perfect timing."

Wade snorted his disagreement.

"We're all set." Stone glanced from Wade to Leah and back again, his brow flexing with concern. "I was just coming to get you. Figured Cookie might've sidelined you with coffee and a snack."

"All I want is a beer," Wade grumbled. "That will wait until we're done."

"I'll buy." Stone gave Leah a smile. "You in?"

"What I want most is a long, indulgent spa day," she said. "Which will also wait."

Stone chuckled but Wade's head filled with images of Leah being pampered. By him. It was the small thread of tension and doubt in her voice that kept him silent. Subtle enough he was sure Stone wouldn't pick up on it. But Wade had just finished a crash course on Leah Williams and he understood all the little nuances.

She was stressed. Almost more now than before they'd moved on the breeding operation. Was it about him or the meeting? Both, probably. Given a choice, he would have asked Stone to put this off for a day or two, but for Leah, he suspected the sooner they got this over with the better.

When this was over and behind them, they could dig into the things he wanted to discuss. The things he needed to share, before he lost the opportunity.

Seeing the video conference set up, Wade shoved all the personal concerns aside in favor of business. Two of the three men currently on camera were unfamiliar to Wade. He recognized Hank Patterson and said hello. Once he and Leah were situated, the introductions were made.

"Hello, Wade. It's good to see you," Hank began. "And a pleasure to meet you, Leah. Wade, I'm joined by Patrick Gamble and Nolan Swann." Both men waved in turn, clearly well-acquainted with Hank. "Gamble and Swann are legal counsel for the Guardian Agency and equally invested in how the two of you identified and brought down the illegal breeder."

Wade gave Leah a nod.

"Together," Leah said. After a deep breath, she explained spotting Tyson in West Yellowstone and her discovery of the ambush on the wolf pack. Taking turns, they filled in the details of the chase, the murder they'd witnessed, as well as the take-down and recovery of the wolves. Stone provided the latest information from the sheriff to wrap up the report.

"You've done a phenomenal job, Leah," Gamble said. "Thank you for the assist, Wade. Let me assure you, no one involved with this illegal breeding operation will be roaming free anytime soon," Gamble promised.

"We have your comprehensive statements and the men who ambushed the wolf pack are turning on each other as well," Swann said. "Thanks to the documents you found at the site, our research team is tracking down the clients and animals," he added. "The next delivery was scheduled for next week. They had a charter flight planned from Cody Regional Airport to Los Angeles."

Leah glanced at him, eyes wide. Turning back to their audience she said, "I don't want to think about those animals in LA."

"Now you don't have to," Wade soothed. He reached over and squeezed her hand hoping the move wasn't too obvious to their superiors on camera. "You found them and put an end to the operation."

"Our agency has excellent protectors," Swann said with pride. "We have a team coordinating with law enforcement in northern Indiana to crash on the relay point where researchers learned several hybrids were being held."

"We're confident they will roll on whatever remains of the operation," Gamble said. "Our personnel are tracing the money so no one involved will slip through the cracks."

The lawyers praised Leah for her effort and dedication and thanked Wade again for providing backup and keeping her safe throughout the ordeal. "It was good to see you, Hank," Gamble said. "We appreciate another assist. All the best to your family."

"You've coordinated on other operations?" Wade asked. Leah valued her career. He wanted that for her. But maybe there was a happy medium, a place where they could be together, both of them doing their best work.

"We have a few mutual acquaintances," Hank replied. Gamble and Swann both smiled enigmatically.

"And it's always good to have friends in the right places," Gamble said before the lawyers signed off.

When the video call ended, Stone shook Wade's hand and gave Leah a brisk hug. "You're off the rotation for at least a week," he said to Wade. "As for you Leah, I'm sure Chelsea is looking forward to seeing you before you head off."

"Right." Leah's smile was a faint shadow of the normal vibrant expression.

"No one holds it against you," Stone continued. "Around here we definitely understand what it means to be undercover or keep certain things private. Chelsea swears you're one of the best employees at the center. You seem to put your all into whatever you do. That's a trait everyone appreciates."

"Thanks," she said, eyeing the door.

Wade could see the words weren't sinking in. "Why don't I take you home?" he offered.

"Great." Her voice was flat. "That would be great."

It wasn't until they were outside and she was climbing into his truck that she abruptly stopped. "Not home. My car is at the research center and I'll need it."

To leave town, no doubt. "Sure." He smothered the frustration gathering in his chest. "Let's go get your car."

She hadn't made any secret of the travel involved in her Guardian Agency career. He'd been foolishly hoping that what had happened between them changed something. Her outlook, her perspective. But how could he ask her to change anything when he hadn't told her exactly how he felt?

$\sim$

"So, what's next?"

Wade's question startled her out of her gloomy thoughts as he pulled into the parking space beside her car.

The research center was closed. Her car and his truck were the only vehicles in the lot. The two of them, alone again. There was a strange sense of comfort in that sense of being apart from every-thing and everyone. That isolation was where they knew each other best. But it was over and she had no idea what came next.

She pressed her lips together. Hard. What she wanted—to stay close to Wade for the rest of her days—sounded lame and clingy, even in her own head. Would've been too easy to beg him to spend the night and the night after that. She had no idea where the healthy boundary might be. Did he need time or some space? Did she? They'd been joined at the hip pretty much since they'd met out there in the woods. Taking a break might be smart.

Except being apart from Wade felt all wrong. Her palms turned damp and her breath caught in her throat just thinking about walking into her empty apartment.

She blamed her sudden lack of independence on the weariness dragging at her body and the crisis they'd survived because they'd worked *together*. Side by side, they'd navigated a hellacious journey in search of justice. It was more pragmatic to assume that what happened in Yellowstone should stay in Yellowstone. The deep and tender intimacy born during such high stakes couldn't last back in the real world, could it? They should prob-ably start over. At the very least, she should dial back her expectations in order to salvage any future relationship.

"Leah?"

"I don't know," she confessed, trying to be brave when her heart seemed as fragile as blown glass. Wade didn't owe her anything. He certainly didn't deserve her assumptions or wild fantasies about staying together.

Her bosses wouldn't need her here in West Yellowstone, not now. And not with the Brotherhood Protectors in place.

"We solved the case," she murmured.

Once her report was turned in, the Guardian Agency would likely send her to a new client or case. Maybe back to the rodeo. After days on the move, traveling with the client didn't sound nearly as appealing anymore, despite being the smart professional choice. Staying here, close to Wade, meant upending her career path. Again.

Her heart jumped, insistent that Wade was worth it.

"We did," he agreed.

"You know my actual employer is based in Chicago." She clamped her lips shut before she dumped her messy, mushy feelings all over him.

"Is that your way of saying you're leaving the area?"

Her throat went tight. "Unless they have another client nearby," she managed. "I'll probably take some time to see my parents. They'll want to hear all the details firsthand."

"I'm sure." Wade's lips tilted into a faint smile. "They'll be so proud of you," he said. "You could come back." He rested his hands at the top of the steering wheel. "There's a protection agency right here. I'm sure they'd be happy to put your expertise to good use."

"They have plenty of experts already. Like you," she said.

Asking Stone for a job felt a little too forward, especially since she hadn't even spoken with her own employers about her options yet. Gamble and Swann had saved her and given her a way to contribute beyond merely making a living. She wouldn't cheapen that by walking away without a word. Besides, she had zero military experience, unlike the entirety of the growing Yellowstone Brotherhood Protectors team. Wade's familiar scowl clouded his eyes, deepening the lines etched on his brow and bracketing his mouth. Why did she find that so endearing? More importantly, why did she feel compelled to ease that expression and tease a smile out of him?

Because she loved him.

She was crazy about him. Not a passing phase or momentary fascination. In. Love. She respected his skills and commitment, enjoyed his sense of humor and admired his tenacity to pursue what was right, no matter the odds.

And yet she was willing to keep all that inside

and walk away from the best relationship she'd ever had? Assuming the chase through the wilderness and takedown of the breeder met the definition of relationship.

"I won't keep you," she said. "Thanks for the ride." She shifted toward him, seeking some sort of physical farewell.

He caught her hand in his. "Why not?" he demanded, his voice low and sharp.

"I beg your pardon?"

"No. Don't do that." His gaze narrowed. "Don't pretend like you don't know what I'm talking about."

But she didn't. "Wade, I don't know what you want me to say."

"Tell me why you won't keep me."

The intensity in his gorgeous eyes, eyes she'd come to love, held her hostage. She couldn't look away. "I meant I won't keep you here. Tonight. I must be wasting your time. You have other things to do. Other places to be," she said in a rush.

"Other people to rescue?"

It felt like he was taunting her. Her shoulders stiffened. "I'm sure in time, yes."

"And what if I come back from one of those rescues and I want you? Need you." He rubbed the bridge of his nose. "You know my work is hard and the happy ending isn't guaranteed."

"You crave the challenges and the successful rescues far outweigh the others," she soothed.

"I'm not keeping score." His frustration was palpable. "True, I thrive on a challenge. I don't see that changing. But, Leah, I've learned there are rescue efforts that leave an indelible mark."

"Your dad."

He reached over and smoothed her hair behind her ear. "Yes. The rescue and loss set me on this path. But I'm talking about you. You mean everything, Leah. When we were out there, I knew losing you would break me. More than anything, I want you to keep me. Keep us. I love you. And I think you love me."

Keep us. The words echoed in her heart as her pulse thundered in her ears. She wasn't breathing properly at all. Back in that ranger station, when it felt as if they were the only two people in the world, she would've sworn that love was possible. Not just possible, but present and real. Her connection with Wade had been too special, too deep, to be anything easily dismissed and forgotten.

"I am in love with you, Wade." Her breath came easier after she got the words out. She pushed at her hair. "You're so much braver than me." The urge to reach for him, to draw on his strength one more time was nearly irresistible. "Are you sure you want to tell a coward you love her?"

"Absolutely. If it means you don't run away. If it

means I get to keep you. We're good together, Leah. More than that, I'm all in here. If Chicago is where you need to be, let's go together. I can find work there."

"You can find work anywhere," she agreed. "But your place is here. Your team would hate me if I dragged you away."

He shook his head. "They'd be happy for me," he countered. "Because they'd know that by following you, I'm following my heart."

He was acting like it would be easy. It terrified her. "I love you, Wade." She rubbed her thumb over her racing pulse at her wrist. "Staying together, keeping one another? That all sounds like heaven. Like the fantasy that was so out of reach I didn't even dare to dream about it."

"Dare," he said. "Dream with me. I went out to find a lost employee for Chelsea on Stone's orders. Instead, I found you, and you've changed my entire outlook on what the future can be. What I can be.

"We can sort out things with your bosses or mine. I understand your loyalty and respect it. Your bosses have worked with Hank's teams time and again. There has to be a middle ground. Maybe you can be a floater."

She laughed. "Such an appealing title for a career."

He smiled and her heart warmed. "The career

that matters to me? The title I want most is to be yours, Leah. That's all."

Shifting in her seat, she leaned over the console and kissed him soundly. Everything fell into place with a soft sigh.

"That's better," he said against her lips. "A fair start." He brushed her hair out of her eyes with a tender touch and traced the line of her jaw. "You'll have to marry me. I need that binding, legal commitment. Paperwork is kind of my thing. I'm not leaving any loopholes for you to escape."

The declaration was so ridiculous she laughed again, her forehead dropping to his shoulder. "Stop teasing me. As if I'd ever want to escape. Through a loophole or otherwise. I love you, you big scowly hunk. Come on." She sat back and pushed open her door. "Let's go to my place and I'll show you how much."

"Leah." The scowl she'd mentioned returned, underscoring his grumbling tone. The man was a grizzly bear in the wrong body sometimes. And he loved her. It was a marvel.

"I'm not teasing." He climbed out of the truck, watching her through the windshield as he walked to her side. Opening her door, he reached into the glove box, rooting around until he pulled out a keyring. He removed the keys and dropped to one knee, holding up the metal circlet. "I'm not teasing," he said again. "Be my wife, Leah. Please marry me. Build a life with me."

"Wade." She clapped her hands over her mouth, blinking away the sudden rush of tears.

"Please, don't cry. We'll find a better ring before I meet your parents."

Her hands fell to her lap as she laughed. "You're serious."

"There's no one else for me," he said. "In a crisis or in a parking lot. In town or out there in the wilderness. Say, yes, Leah. Please."

"But…but, Wade, this is so sudden. Shouldn't we take some time?"

"If you need time." His mouth firmed as if he was trying to hold back. Then the dam burst. "I won't rush you. But for me…" His voice trailed off. "Well, I can't bear the thought of taking time without a good reason. Life doesn't come with a guarantee. I can't tell you how many times in the last few days that worry for you, your safety, nearly took me out at the knees."

"I'm not a child," she said, thinking back to the first meal they'd shared in that ranger station. He smiled. "No, you're not. I've seen how capable you are. I love your strength, inside and out. But, sweetheart, life is sudden." Standing up, he ran a hand over her silky hair. "Can you really sit there and tell me things didn't change for you while we were out there?"

"Of course not." She leaned into his touch, savored the security and affection coursing through her body when he was near. She'd never been so close to anything as lovely and full of promise. "Everything changed. From the moment you found me," she whispered.

She took the silly excuse for a ring, turning it between her fingers. Finally, she looked up into his warm brown eyes. That was love she saw in his gaze. Steady, exciting, and lasting love. "Yes, Wade. Yes. It will be a joy and an honor to be your wife."

He tipped up her chin and kissed her. Claimed her. His lips were warm, his calloused hands gentle as he cradled her face.

"Can I go with you to visit your parents?"

"Want to make the most of your week off?"

"Definitely," he said. "We can stop by a court-house and make it official."

Her parents might have an opinion on that. She was certain his family would want to be present when he exchanged vows. Not to mention his team and the Brotherhood Protector family he'd joined. "Maybe," she hedged. "Thanksgiving is just around the corner. Do you have traditions?"

"Are you kidding? For years, Army tradition was being assigned somewhere and enjoying a turkey dinner with all the trimmings in the DFAC. Dining facility," he clarified.

"Before that. Don't you want to go home and see your mom?"

"I'd spoil her fun," he said. "Her first empty-nest holiday season hit her hard and after that, she came up with some fascinating combination of Friends-giving and an extended girls' weekend. It's a whole thing." He waved it away. "You can ask her about it eventually. Let's create our own traditions. Starting this year," he said. "I'm thankful for you, Leah. I want to spend every day making you happy."

Her whole body tingled with happiness, like a bottle of champagne ready to pop the cork. Her joy, so pure and bright, sparkled through her as she imagined a future that was entirely new and fresh. "Wade." For a moment that was all she could say. She swallowed, searching for her courage. "I'd given up on finding someone like you."

"Someone scowly?" he joked.

She shook her head. "Someone amazing. Someone special. You listened when it mattered most." She touched his lips when he started to interrupt. She needed to get all of this out. No one understood her, supported her like Wade. "You encouraged me to trust my instincts. You never gave me a chance to doubt myself. You're the one person I trust with all of me. I love you so much."

He wrapped her in his arms. Being held by him was the best feeling in the world.

"I love you, too," he said. "You're the best thing that's ever happened to me."

"Let's go tell Justice," she suggested.

"In due time. He reminded me recently that Mom shouldn't be the last to know. Let's clean up and then we can do a video chat intro."

"Oh." He was moving at lightning speed, but she didn't hate it. "Think she'll like me?"

"Sweetheart, she'll fall in love with you faster than I did."

How did he make every minute happier for her than the last? Love, she decided as they walked toward her apartment, her heart soaring with hope, joy, and the promises of their future together.

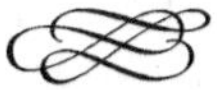

"TEN MINUTES TO MIDNIGHT!" Stone's voice boomed through the lodge. He and Kyla wound through the crowd toward a table loaded with chilled bottles of champagne to help fill glasses for everyone.

The lodge was overflowing with Brotherhood Protectors, their partners, and plenty of friends.

A moment later, Wade saw Hannah and Nate move to help Stone and Kyla. Across the room, Gabe and Harper were playing cards with Alex and Eris. Wade wasn't sure what the game was, but it was clear from the laughter they were all having a great time.

New Year's Eve in West Yellowstone was a lot more exciting than Wade had anticipated. Parties had never been his thing and he'd tried to avoid this one. Loving Leah was so new, that his default was to keep her all to himself. But Leah, along with his brother and the rest of their teammates, were all in for tonight's celebration.

Within minutes of arriving, Wade realized they'd all been right. His team had moved here together, eager to make a positive impact. And they'd done that, tackling some high profile situations and successfully managing a variety of crises already.

But each of them had also found so much more than satisfying work. He'd watched the changes as Gabe, Nate, Alex, and Justice had discovered a sense of peace along with that purpose. They'd each found the love that lasts with remarkable women.

As part of the larger team of Brotherhood Protectors, they'd created something more than the typical definition of a community. Somehow, they'd all managed to blend into a family. A big, noisy, extended family Wade could count on to celebrate the highs and walk with him through the lows of life.

For the guy who'd planned to limit the close relationships in his life, it was a brand-new outlook. An outlook that was much easier to embrace with Leah beside him. He brushed a kiss to her temple, delighted as always when she leaned into him.

"Five minutes!" Stone called out.

The crowd milled about in excitement and Wade glanced at Justice. "You want beer or champagne?"

"After the year we've had? It's definitely champagne time." With his arm around Payton, Justice gave her a squeeze. "What about you?"

"I vote for bubbly," Payton replied with a big smile.

"Me too," Leah chimed in. She pressed on her toes to kiss his jaw. "Need a hand?"

"I've got it," he assured her. He wound his way to the table and returned with four glasses, just as Stone declared one minute to go.

The last few seconds of the year ticked away with everyone counting down in joyful unison. Minding the champagne glasses, he gathered Leah into his arms. "You ready for this?" he asked.

"I'm ready for anything, as long as we're in it together."

A chorus of "Happy New Year" cheers mixed with a storm of streamers, poppers, and colorful confetti.

Surrounded by chaos, Wade kissed Leah. That's all it took to quiet everything in his heart and mind. She was his miracle, the woman he'd found, the woman he loved, and the woman he couldn't wait to grow with through the years to come.

"Happy New Year, my love," he said for her ears alone.

She beamed at him, her brown eyes sparkling. "Happy New Year, Wade."

All around them, his teammates were doing the same with their partners. His heart overflowed with happiness and a contentment he hadn't known he needed.

Brotherhood Protectors Yellowstone World
Team Wolf
Guarding Harper - Desiree Holt
Guarding Hannah - Delilah Devlin
Guarding Eris - Reina Torres
Guarding Payton - Jen Talty
Guarding Leah - Regan Black

ABOUT REGAN BLACK

Regan Black, a USA Today and internationally bestselling author, writes award-winning, action-packed romances featuring kick-butt heroines and the sexy heroes who fall in love with them. Raised in the Midwest and California, she and her husband share their empty nest with two adorably arrogant cats in the South Carolina Lowcountry where the rich blend of legend, romance, and history fuels her imagination.

For free reads, exclusive prizes, and much more, subscribe to the monthly newsletter at Regan-Black.com/perks.

Keep up with Regan online:
www.ReganBlack.com
Facebook
Instagram

Or follow Regan on:
BookBub
Amazon

Sandman

Death-Trap Date

Last Strike

Mirage

Unknown Identities - Brotherhood Protectors crossover novellas:

Moving Target

Lost Signal

Off The Radar

For full details on all of Regan's books visit ReganBlack.com and

enjoy excerpts from each of her sexy, adrenaline-fueled novels.

Deadly Observations

Deadly Reflections, Behind Closed Doors series

Black Ice, Stormwatch series

what she knew, Breakdown Book 4, a multi-author series

Knight Traveler Series

The Matchmaker Series

Escape Club Heroes, Harlequin Romantic Suspense

The Riley Code, Harlequin Romantic Suspense

Colton Family saga, a multi-author series, Harlequin Romantic Suspense

ABOUT ELLE JAMES

ELLE JAMES also writing as MYLA JACKSON is a *New York Times* and *USA Today* Bestselling author of books including cowboys, intrigues and paranormal adventures that keep her readers on the edges of their seats. When she's not at her computer, she's traveling, snow skiing, boating, or riding her ATV, dreaming up new stories. Learn more about Elle James at www.ellejames.com

Website | Facebook | Twitter | GoodReads | Newsletter | BookBub | Amazon

Or visit her alter ego Myla Jackson at mylajackson.com
Website | Facebook | Twitter | Newsletter

Follow Me!
www.ellejames.com
ellejamesauthor@gmail.com